PRIMORDIAL

The Ethereals Series

Book One

CHIA L. STRICKLAND

"Every great dream begins with a
dreamer. Always remember, you have
within you the strength, the patience,
and the passion to reach for the stars
to change the world."
Harriet Tubman

This one is for all the dreamers.

Prologue

SHE COULD FEEL THE dew-soaked grass between her toes as she ran headfirst through the labyrinth of twigs and branches. She'd lost them long ago, unsure whether or not their pursuit of her had come to a halt or if this was a new tactic, a diversion. She slowed down to regulate her breathing — her breath forming small clouds of mist in the cold morning air. She glanced behind her as she continued at the slower pace — a stolen look over her left shoulder then one over her right, though there was little she could make out in the dark. The thumping of her feet against the ground matched that of her racing heart. With her anxiety growing, she increased her speed once more.

They would not catch her, not tonight. Not ever. She was destined for more than this and she knew it. They knew it. She refused to look back again — she needed to concentrate. All her energy would be required to get through this. Desperation began to slowly twirl its way around her spine but she ignored it before it could take hold. Doubt was a luxury she couldn't afford. She pushed her anxiety as far down as she could force it. She would make it out — she didn't have any other choice. Every stride felt like an eternity away from safety as she sprinted through the pitch-black woods.

The earth around her seemed to purr, releasing vibrations that pulsated into and through her bones as a clearing came into view. Violent wind whipped her hair across her face, further obscuring her already limited vision. She could feel them coming for her now, faster than they had been chasing her before. Their power tingled on her skin as they approached, circling her from the shadows — the respite from their hunt had been a distraction and now she was surrounded. She stopped moving and squinted through the darkness. They were closing in on her. Close, but far enough that she might still escape if she played her cards right. Maybe if they underestimated her just enough, she could make it through the clearing to safety. She stepped forward and took a deep breath — the scent of damp earth comforted her; the crisp air made her more alert. She relaxed her jaw, rolled her shoulders back and prepared herself for the final sprint to freedom.

But the grass that consoled her before peeled back — it was no friend to her now. The ground opened its mouth hungrily, devouring her whole. She was gone *and the only thing left of her existence was the echo of her scream.*

I

Impossible

SAWYER

IT DIDN'T TAKE TOO long for her to realize that the screams assaulting her ears were her own. She stopped screaming, sat up, and looked around the room with its unsettling darkness. The realization that she was familiar with her environment started to slow down her accelerated heart rate. Her laptop was still open where she'd left it on the desk, and the bathroom's soft mood lighting was peeking out from behind the closed door. Sawyer ran her hand over her sheets, touching the fabric as a way to confirm that her surroundings were real. She was fine. Safe. She checked the clock on her side table, sighed, and rolled out of bed, ready to begin her month-old post-nightmare routine.

If she was being honest, she'd grown to enjoy this time of day over the last month — when she didn't count the nightmares. The first few hours of morning after midnight meant very few of her sorority sisters were home — the parties from the night before, still keeping the majority of them entertained somewhere. She stepped into her shower and welcomed the soothing hot water against her skin. Her housemates would begin trickling home with the blue hour sky, and soon enough, her treasured quiet would be no more.

Fifteen minutes later, she was clean and dressed in a fresh set of pajamas — the unease from earlier washed away down the shower drain. Stretched out across her bed with a textbook in hand, Sawyer became absorbed in her thoughts as the motivation to study slipped through her fingers. She lost herself to the world of dream analysis, thoughts of ex-boyfriends, and the dissection of the fickle nature of human beings, until sleep embraced her.

"Wake up!"

Sawyer rolled on to her stomach and groaned as she tried to dodge the fractured sunbeams obnoxiously streaming through the windows. When avoiding the rays of light didn't work, she sat up and stared directly at her suite mate, rubbing the sleep from her eyes to clear her vision. Running her fingers through her hair, she sighed at her friend in annoyance, twisting her fading silk press into a scrunchie.

"Tell me what you want or let me go back to sleep," Sawyer grumbled, and sliding back into a lying position, took an unused pillow to partially smother her head.

"Morning grumpy!" Maddie threw herself on top of Sawyer, the trajectory causing Sawyer to bounce a little when their bodies collided.

Maddelena, affectionately called Maddie, was much thinner and taller than Sawyer, with deep auburn curls that she kept straightened more often than not. Her almond-shaped eyes were dark brown and always accentuated by black volume lashes and cat eye eyeliner. With golden brown skin and full lips which never went without her signature sheer, "pucker-up" lip gloss, she sported over 12 piercings and three tiny hidden tattoos —

one of which was the complementary half to the only, also hidden, tattoo Sawyer had ever gotten.

Sawyer wriggled free and got out of bed, grumbling under her breath as she went.

"You still down to go tonight, right?" Maddie asked, still sprawled across the rumpled comforter.

Sawyer walked into the bathroom and stared at her reflection in the mirror. She was now actively regretting the yes she'd given Maddie last week. Recently, she'd grown bored of parties, and exasperated with the small talk that accompanied men hitting on her. A month ago, she would have been excited to be out, but now, the idea of sweaty bodies everywhere, the DJs who played the same music over and over, and the cheap alcohol were added reasons why she didn't want to go. Her ideal night had morphed into applying a face mask to prep for her movie binge with a glass of wine. Unfortunately, her friends didn't get the memo yet and remained dedicated to pestering her into participating. Sawyer had been working on building boundaries by declining their invitations more, but occasionally, she would give in just to decrease their incessant whining.

"If I *have* to. I'd forgotten that was tonight, to be honest," she sighed before splashing some water on her face. "But I suppose a promise is a promise."

Readjusting the scrunchie to pull her hair into a high ponytail, she inspected the areas where her natural curl pattern was coming back.

Maddie squealed with excitement before catapulting herself off the bed and towards the bedroom door with a small "eek" as she ushered herself outside.

Sawyer rolled her eyes, then plugged in her styling brush so she could touch up her hair. She walked into her closet to find something to wear while she let it heat up. It was going to be a long Saturday now that she hadn't backed out of their plans. Maybe she was being a lot more dramatic than she needed to be. It was just a party, and if she really didn't end up having a good — or at least a decent — time, she could always leave. She felt a little better after her perception of the situation had slightly shifted and headed back to the sink to brush her teeth, watching the previously blinking red light on the brush turn solid, signifying that it was now hot enough to use.

She stood in an unwelcoming vacuum of silence — the only sound, her breathing; her gaze unable to clearly see beyond the outlines of massive trees in the forested area. A soft breeze blew the leafy branches around in silent susurration. The quiescence, a facade to the unease she felt and the feeling of dread she wasn't able to shake. Her heart pounded in her ears like a Lambeg drum as the feeling of trepidation wrapped around her throat in its attempt to strangle her. If this feeling was any indication of what was going to happen tonight, they would finally have her. If the ground didn't swallow her first.

Her feet welcomed the cool grass as they always did, while the Lambeg's ongoing solo made her ears throb. Her blood rushed through her veins like white water rapids — its heat spreading across her face and warming her already pulsating ears. Just a little more Sawyer, just a little more, just like before. *But she wasn't as calm as she had been the last time — as calm as she'd been many times before. Anxiety slithered its way up her arms, making her skin tingle until it itched. But she refused to fidget in case they were watching her, unwilling to show any sign of weakness. It didn't matter that she was afraid, Sawyer wouldn't give them that satisfaction of knowing that she was.*

She took a deep breath, then took off in a sprint, slapping the thinner, stray branches out of her face as she moved through the forest — pushing away any outstretched parts of foliage she could see before they snagged her hair or clothes.

She had been running for a while now and could feel her legs beginning to wobble, but she would not stop and kept pushing through the dips in her strides. The clouds above partially cleared and soft moonlight illuminated the forest, casting elongated shadows of warped shapes throughout the woodland. In the distance, to her right, she could have sworn she caught a brief glimpse of something bright blue running alongside her. But when she looked again, it was gone. Sawyer shook her head and tried to run even faster, her breath refusing to regulate now that her anxiety was morphing into full-blown panic. She ran until her foot got tangled in a protruding root and she hit the ground hard.

Sawyer startled awake and ran to her bathroom, barely making it to the toilet before she threw up. Her head was pounding, her body hurt, and she was clammy with sweat despite the bone-deep chill making her shiver. She decided a shower might help relieve some of her symptoms, the hot water for her muscle pain and the steam for her incoming congestion. Twenty minutes later, Sawyer barely made it back to bed after she'd popped two ibuprofens with half a litre of bottled water, before drifting back to sleep.

"Hey, wake up,"

Through the splitting headache, she was having a serious case of déjà vu. Obviously unaware of asking for a daily wake up call.

"Hey, are you okay?"

Sawyer was groggy and it took a minute for her silence to transform into a groan.

Maddie, who had now sat down at the foot of her bed, started trying to nudge her awake. Sawyer's eyes remained closed; she didn't want to open them — the sunlight was already assaulting her as it streamed through the window next to her bed.

"I need to sleep — my head hurts and I have a fever." The words were half croak, half whisper, as Sawyer struggled to readjust herself without aggravating her headache. She hadn't even realized she had started dozing off until she heard Maddie talking to someone.

"She looks pretty rough, and can't stay awake long enough to have a conversation."

"She hasn't gotten up at all?"

"Did she take something? What happened at the party? Should we get her to a doctor?"

Sawyer opened her eyes, mumbling for help as she tried reaching for the rest of the water on her nightstand, and Shaina, one of the girls with

Maddie, handed her the bottle. She took a sip, using the water to soothe her chapped, overheated lips, and cleared her throat. Securing the nearly empty water bottle, she slowly moved herself into a seated position, every movement sending a searing pain through the middle of her skull.

"I feel like shit," pointing to the pill bottle, she added, "Hand me two more of those and can I have some more water?"

Shaina handed her the pills and Allison, the third girl in the room, left to get a new bottle of water and some orange juice. When Allison came back, cradled in her arms were a number of supplies: more ibuprofen, a cold compress, orange juice, the water, and a thermometer.

"Figured these would help. We should also check her temp just in case," she said, dumping everything on the bed before sitting down.

Sawyer placed the cold compress on the top of her head and took a swig of orange juice as Maddie held the infrared thermometer to her forehead and waited for the beep.

"This is—, we need to—Hospital. *Now!*" Maddie stumbled over her words as she started grabbing random pieces of clothing, shoving them into a large handbag.

"Anything else you need; we can bring it over later. Help her get dressed. We need to go," she instructed Shaina and Allison as she bustled around the room.

She was sure Maddie was being overdramatic, so Sawyer reached over to grab the thermometer, pointing it at her head so she could read it for herself.

"That's impossible." She looked at the blinking red light before it faded again. There's no way. She checked again for good measure, waiting for the telltale sign of the temperature reading.

Beep.

The other three girls exchanged glances, then looked back at the thermometer, a small '163' flashing on the bright red screen.

Holy hell.

2

Open Up

THE THERMOMETER WAS BROKEN, it had to be, but she felt awful so they all agreed she should go to the hospital. Maddie, Allison, and Shaina helped her get dressed and grabbed some more cold compresses before they left. Fingers crossed it was the flu, or something minor they could treat with antibiotics. But realistically, if her temperature was that high, she wouldn't even be alive. Her head hurt so bad she wanted to throw up again. Maddie insisted on repetitively checking her temperature every few minutes as they drove to the hospital. Leaning over, she raised the thermometer to Sawyer's head.

Beep. Two hundred and thirteen.

"I told you it's broken," Sawyer said, taking another sip of water and adding pressure to the cold compress positioned behind her neck.

No one responded as they pulled into a parking spot in the emergency room lot. Soon, they were sitting in a packed reception area waiting for Sawyer's name to be called.

They had been there for so long, she would have been frustrated if she wasn't so extremely fatigued. But right now, there wasn't much more she could do — she was falling apart so she had to stay. The only other option was leaving in hopes of finding an emptier hospital.

"I'm okay enough, I don't think any of you need to stay. I'll call after I see a doctor and see what's going on. I promise."

Allison and Shaina got up hesitantly, before leaving the lobby. Maddie didn't move at all.

"You already know I'm not trynna leave you here like this, Sawce," Maddie looked over at her with a sad smile, squeezing her hand before turning back to her phone screen.

A nurse in peach scrubs was calling her name. Taking a deep breath, she looked up at the woman waving her over. The nurse was standing next to a wheelchair, and insisted Sawyer sit down as soon as she reached her; Maddie was right behind them.

"As you can see, we're quite busy right now, so we'll get her checked in and let you know when you can come back, 'kay hon?" the nurse explained to Maddie, gently nudging her back to the waiting area.

Maddie nodded and gave Sawyer a quick hug, going back to her seat while Sawyer was pushed through the swinging doors and taken to a triage room. Closing the curtain behind her, the nurse pulled out a tablet and began taking vitals.

"Heart and respiration rates are a little elevated, but blood pressure is okay. How are you feeling?" She reached for the thermometer.

"Like I got hit by a train," Sawyer managed to get out before the thermometer was in her mouth. The nurse offered her a small smile.

The thermometer vibrated softly between her lips and the screen of the tablet lit up. The nurse reached out to retrieve the thermometer, glancing down at the tablet screen, confusion marring her face.

"This can't be right. Let me try a new one." She grabbed a new thermometer from a drawer and took a couple minutes to calibrate it to the tablet. "I'm gonna have you place this one under the arm, hon."

Sawyer followed instructions and they both waited for the thermometer's routine. Seconds later, Sawyer felt the tiny vibration which caused the nurse to pause her note taking on the tablet, triple checking the device.

"I'm not sure what's going on, but your temperature isn't being recorded correctly. This — this isn't medically possible." The nurse paused, pushing up her glasses, and took some more notes.

"A doctor will be in to see you shortly — I'll be back with something for your fever." And just like that, Sawyer was alone.

Her nerves were getting the best of her as she waited for a doctor to show up, the soft ticks of the clock were the only sound in the room apart from the air kicking on and off. The nurse hadn't explicitly *said* she worried about Sawyer's temperature, but her abrupt departure did. The short, stocky woman had gotten confused, then a tad flustered, and rushed out of the triage area to find someone to help.

She was still freezing and the air conditioning in the hospital wasn't helping. Her body throbbed in places she didn't know she could throb, and, mentally and emotionally, Sawyer was feeling somewhat overwhelmed. The more time she spent waiting, the more paranoid she became. She picked up the thermometer that the nurse had left behind and shoved it into her mouth. *I'm gonna be fine. It can't be that bad.* Her thoughts were interrupted by the light vibration. She glanced down. Two hundred and fifty-three.

I'm gonna die.

The curtain opened up and Sawyer quickly wiped the tear running down her left cheek. The nurse was back with a doctor. He smiled and explained that they were going to admit her to the hospital for observation and administer a drip to keep her hydrated while they ran some tests.

"Nurse Etta will take you up and get you comfortable, then I'll be back. Don't worry, you're in good hands." He smiled before ducking out and pulling the curtain close.

Sawyer gingerly climbed into the provided wheelchair. Soon, she was being transported to her room after her hospital admission was complete. And shortly after that, Maddie was at her bedside.

"Did they say how long you'd be here? I should call your parents, right?" she gushed nervously.

"No, don't call my parents! It might not be that bad." Maddie tilted her head and raised her right brow at Sawyer. "And no, they didn't say." Sawyer exhaled loudly, running her hand down her face. "I just don't want to worry them until we're sure there's something to worry about.

Maddie reached into her giant handbag and handed Sawyer the sweater she'd grabbed earlier.

"Tell you what — I'll go grab some more of your things; I won't forget your phone this time and I'll let the house know you won't be back for a while. By the time I get back, at least some of the tests should be done. Right?"

"Right."

"Okay, we wait. *Then* we'll call your parents if we have to. But hopefully we won't." Maddie stood, preparing to leave.

She turned back to her when she got to the door, a sympathetic smile on her face, eyes filled with worry. Sawyer tried her best to fake a Duchenne smile, hating to see her friend so concerned.

"Love ya, lady! Be back soon." She made a heart with her hands and stuck her tongue out at Maddie, who rewarded her with a laugh as she left the room.

Half an hour later, Sawyer had met more doctors than she'd seen her entire life, and had her blood drawn too many times to keep track. She appreciated the drips, which did help. But after the latest dose of medication refused to work, the doctors decided to go the unconventional route, trying therapeutic hypothermia via frequent ice baths to keep her fever from getting worse. She heard "specialist" and "medical anomaly" mentioned on and off, as doctors and nurses came and went from her room.

She was dozing off when the sound of the opening door startled her awake. Two women entered, one softly closed the door behind them, and the other started to approach her. She couldn't tell what their role was — neither looked like the nurses nor doctors she'd spent the last 45 minutes meeting. And their outfits, besides the lab coats, were not acceptable on duty hospital wear.

One woman was dressed in thigh-high, leather boots and distressed denim shorts. She wore a ripped tee — cut just above her stomach — and had a white coat thrown over the ensemble. She had very fluffy, curly hair that started dark brown at the roots but faded into a light, golden-brown ombré, the ends were almost blonde. She was slim and tall, and with her deep brown skin, she was one of the prettiest women Sawyer had ever seen. She walked into the room and propped herself against the wall next to the door frame.

The other woman, who followed behind her, was just as stunning. She closed the door once she'd entered the room. Wearing a skintight dress, and a white coat with a stethoscope around her neck. Her hair was a congregation of wild sun-kissed curls — a combination of browns, blondes and reds. It bounced as she walked towards the bed, and Sawyer noticed the childlike twinkle in her eyes that seemed to soften her entire face.

"Oirt, check she temperature quick cause we ain' got a lotta time." The first woman was saying from her position, where she kept subtly lifting up the side of the shade to peep through the transom of the hospital door.

"Relax, it's gonna take a minute."

"Ya gotta hurry up."

Sawyer, though concerned, couldn't help smiling at the interaction between the two new-comers. They went back and forth for a little while, and Sawyer realized the second woman was Irish. The first accent was harder to make out — she had no idea where the first lady was from.

For a while, she wasn't sure they were in the right room as she sat watching "Leather

Dress" rummage around. She was about to ask them if they'd had the right place when the scouring stopped.

"Found one!" The Irish woman, "Leather Dress", was making her way towards Sawyer with an infrared thermometer pointed at her head. When she was in range, the telltale beep of the medical instrument sounded.

"Sickner for ya, I told ya!"

"You can't win when ahn even see it. Lemme see!" "Short Shorts" had moved from next to the door. She was trying to grab the thermometer as the other woman kept dodging her attempts by dancing out of reach.

"I'll take my band of cash if you don't mind." "Leather Dress" smirked at "Short Shorts" who was obviously irritated about losing.

Sawyer was caught off guard at the amount, and wondered what kind of idiots would bet that sort of money on something as random as a stranger's temperature. Maybe doctors got paid a lot more than she assumed. And why weren't they addressing her when she was sitting there *obviously* dying? Were *these women* the specialists? Or just two med students who had heard about the medical anomaly and decided to take a look? She wasn't able to deduce anything from what was happening. But before she had the chance to ask all the unanswered questions she'd been mentally compiling, the timer on the nightstand went off, signaling to her that it was time for another dip.

"No for real, stop playing. Gimme de thermometer while you checking de tablet to see if you could access de intake information."

She started to ask what was wrong with her intake information when slender fingers looped around her arm and started dragging her out of bed. "Short Shorts", who was now standing next to Sawyer, forcefully gripped her forearm, watching her partner who was now focused on the tablet.

"Mira, it done?" "Short Shorts" was asking.

Mira, formerly "Leather Dress", didn't respond at first. Then she looked up with a grin of satisfaction.

"It's done." She tossed the tablet back on the tray she'd grabbed it from.

"Short Shorts" turned to look straight into Sawyer's eyes and when she spoke, it was slower, clearer, and with only a hint of the thick accent she had before.

"Just so we understand each other, if you scream, that will be the last sound you ever make."

Stiletto-shaped fingernails dug slightly into her skin; Sawyer nodded faintly, with the realization that the long night ahead of her was just beginning.

Leaving the hospital hadn't been the ordeal Sawyer imagined — at least she could walk a little better than before, and that was preferable to the alternative of possibly being dragged around. "Short Shorts" never let go of her, looping their elbows together so they looked more like friends leaving the emergency room and not a kidnapper and her hostage.

The three of them had exited through a side door and rounded the corner of the building closest to them. They passed three ambulance stations before turning right and ducking through a narrow passageway that opened up into a parking lot. In all, they'd walked for what felt like twenty minutes until they abruptly stopped when a black Range Rover came into view. "Short Shorts" resumed her kidnapper hold instead of the looped-at-the-elbows one, and Mira turned around to face Sawyer — she had been walking in front of them the entire time, leading them to the car. She pulled a small vial from her pocket and shook the pink, iridescent liquid in front of Sawyer.

"Open up." She smiled.

"I am *not* drinking that." Sawyer was happy she sounded more like herself now, despite still being sick.

"Do you want to feel better or not?" Mira looked over at "Short Shorts" for reinforcement.

"Who are you?" Sawyer ignored the pink liquid, looking back and forth as she waited for an answer.

"I know. I know. We don't have time for this. I'll just put it in the back with her. She'll either drink it and feel better or won't drink it and keep feeling like shit." Mira was ignoring her and speaking directly to "Short Shorts".

Then, she was being coaxed forward towards the car. The back door was pulled open.

"I'll owe you a pint for this," then her vision was obscured by a blindfold. Something was tied around her wrists to bind them together.

"You've got to be kidding me."

Another nudge guided her into the vehicle. Sawyer heard her seatbelt click after being dragged across her chest. She was fiddling with the small vile now resting between her hands. She could hear the clicking of heels meeting concrete, two more doors closing, one after the other, and then the purr of the engine.

There was silence for a while after they started moving. Eventually, someone started playing some music, although Sawyer couldn't understand most of the lyrics. Occasionally, she would hear one of the women sporadically singing along, accompanied by faint sounds of laughter.

Sawyer wasn't sure how long it had taken to reach their destination. She had gotten lost somewhere after the sixth left and third right turn, so she knew there was no way for her to get back without help. She wanted to cry. But instead took a deep breath, exhaling slowly through her mouth to prevent her tears from falling. Then the car stopped. They were at their destination, wherever it was.

I'm definitely gonna die.

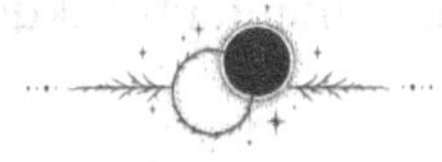

The blindfold had been removed and the zip ties cut, once she was indoors. When Sawyer felt brave enough to open her eyes, she immediately closed them again. *This can't be real.* She wrapped herself in a hug as she stood in the giant foyer and was pinching her arm in an attempt to wake herself up. *I'm still in the hospital and delusional from my fever.* She pulled her arms around herself tighter.

"Um, what is she doing?" She listened to the voices around her. This person was new — a British voice she hadn't heard before.

I could be in a coma from the fever. It's possible.

"I ain' know, girl." That was definitely "Short Shorts" speaking.

"When do you think she's going to open her eyes again?" the first voice asked.

"I ain' just say I ain' know? Ask she." "Short Shorts" replied with a chuckle.

Another voice interrupted the conversation. One that sounded very similar to the British girl asking all the questions.

"Maybe if you two had taken the time to talk to her instead of kidnapping her, she wouldn't be close to having a mental breakdown in the foyer."

"Short Shorts" made a sound with her mouth that Sawyer had never heard before. "Shoulda went yaself den," the woman grumbled.

She couldn't completely understand everything "Short Shorts" said, but from the little time Sawyer had been around her, she seemed perpetually annoyed by everyone and everything.

They bickered back and forth while waiting, as she stood motionless for what seemed like eternity. She had counted to approximately a hundred before she decided she was an adult and had the courage to open her eyes, stumbling backward when she did. Despite nearly falling, her stumble fortunately gave her some breathing space even though she'd accidentally dropped the vial. The small glass object hit the floor and rolled towards the girl standing near her. Sawyer looked at the vial and then glanced around at the people in the room — two women and a teenager — who were all staring back at her.

"Hi, I'm Imogen," said the girl who was standing almost face to face with Sawyer before the stumble. She picked up the vial and offered it to Sawyer as the other two in the room turned their heads towards them. She smiled at Sawyer, giving the container a little twirl. "You're gonna want to drink this."

She looked at the girl and slowly extended her hand to take the vial, although she had no plans to drink the mysterious pink liquid.

"She is hot," Imogen declared when her fingers brushed against Sawyer's during the exchange.

Sawyer withdrew her hand so quickly that if her temperature wasn't close to burning Imogen, the friction from withdrawing her hand so fast would have. She took another step back from where she'd landed when she stumbled, and groaned softly.

"Not to be rude or anything but what's happening? *Who are you people?*" Her questions tumbled out more loudly and frantically than she'd hoped.

It took a little time before Imogen stepped forward, and when she did, it was slowly. She seemed afraid to approach Sawyer, like Sawyer was a piece of fine China she was worried about breaking. Sawyer couldn't help but stare at her and her minute attempts at shifting closer.

That's when she noticed the new woman in the room with them, that and the fact that Mira was missing. The recent addition must have been the second British voice from before; it would make sense that she sounded a lot like Imogen, since she looked a lot like her too. The two of them were nearly the same height and had similar complexions — they looked like carbon copies of each other. But their eyes were different, and their hair was different too. Imogen had waist-length, Bohemian locs, that started with pitch black roots and gradually transitioned in colour until they ended in electric blue.

She had striking blue eyes that stood out against her honey-toned brown skin. The other woman's hair was slightly shorter than Imogen's and from what Sawyer could see, it came to the middle of her back and had light gray, maybe white, highlights which made Sawyer think of a skunk. Sawyer couldn't clearly see the colour of her eyes from where she was standing, but she could tell that they were dark, unlike Imogen's.

Imogen started talking, pulling Sawyer's attention back to her.

"Well, you already know I'm Imogen."

She motioned to the other two individuals in the room, and continued speaking when Sawyer didn't offer up any confirmation.

"This," she pointed to the woman who looked just like her, "is my sister, Anabelle, and *that* is Iyana." This time, she pointed to "Short Shorts", who seemed entirely uninterested in inserting herself into the conversation.

Sawyer opened her mouth to respond, not sure what she was going to say but knowing she had no more patience to spare.

"I would say nice to meet you, except, you merry bunch of criminals have kidnapped me, and I'm pretty sure I'm dying from an unknown disease. I feel like shit and it's possible my fever's gotten so high I'm in a coma, so I don't even know if this is real." She paused to breathe. "And if this isn't a coma and I'm free to leave, then it's been really *really* nice to meet you, but I've got to go. So, if you could just get me back to the—, in fact, nevermind,

I'll get myself back." She started looking around to hopefully spot the way out.

"Wee bit of a drama queen, aren't ye?"

Mira walked into the room chuckling at the tail end of Sawyer's rant. The woman hopped up onto a counter close by, leaned over, and started grabbing drinks. She threw one to everyone, including Sawyer, who made no attempt to catch the can. Shrugging as the drink hit the floor and rolled behind a chair, Mira started off where Imogen ended.

"Before I explain, I just want to say that I understand that this will sound like we are fecking away with the fairies. But give us a chance and drink the liquid in the vial for Pete's sake." She stretched across the counter she was now sitting on.

Sawyer was agitated and lethargic from her illness, so the smile on the woman's face made her instinctively not want to believe whatever Mira was going to say.

"Now it's a lot, and we know yer not likely to believe us because let's face it — most days, I don't believe it either, but yer like us. We're different. Special. I'm, well, it'd be easier for me to show ya." She smiled again and tilted her head in the direction of the house plants, all of which started blooming.

Sawyer didn't believe her eyes. She simply sat down on the floor, speechless. Mira gave her a minute to refocus before she continued talking.

"As you can see, earth's my element. It's also why my hair is like this — don't know why it happens, but I think it works as an identifier. It didn't always look like this." She twisted a curly strand through her fingers. "It used to be just dark brown all over. Then one day, I got really sick and these lot found me. Once I was better, I had these nifty gifts and new hair. It won't change colour now, no matter what I do!"

Sawyer nodded silently, discombobulated by the ongoing experience. Nothing Mira was saying was making any sense to her, but on some level, Sawyer found herself torn between pure denial and considering how much of this information she thought was the truth. The explanation continued before she had a chance to interject.

"Iyana draws her power from the sun — if ye couldn't guess by her crazy mane. The other two over there, Anabelle and Imogen, round out air and water," she happily said before she kept talking. "But yeah, we think yer fire. Isn't that exciting?"

She was giddy with enthusiasm, and resumed her monologue again before Sawyer had a chance to respond.

"We still don't know a lot about why and how we were chosen, or why we can do what we can. But we are sure that you belong here, with us. We're the— "

"Wait. Wait! What is—" Sawyer had enough and finally cut her off before Mira kept her there all day. She struggled to formulate a cohesive thought or sentence at first, "What's….What's your name again? Mira?"

"Oh, sorry. I should have led with that. Only me friends call me that. Name's Amira." She chuckled.

"Okay, Amira, you're telling me that you have the power to manipulate nature? And did *this*?" Sawyer paused to gesture to the now completely bloomed plants and flowers, "Ignoring the fact that that's *completely ludicrous,* and assuming I was somewhat buying this, what does that have to do with me? What makes you so sure I'm like you?"

This time it was Anabelle who answered.

"How many people do you know who can survive a fever over *a hundred and five degrees* without medical intervention? If anything, I'd think that alone would be reason enough to want to know how that's possible, love. And if I were you, I would drink that."

Anabelle glanced at Sawyer's hands, then directly at Sawyer who avoided making eye contact as she flipped the vial incessantly.

"Here's what we know so far. Humans were once entrusted with a few of the universe's powers and were tasked with the job of maintaining the natural balance. Every human had just a little bit of universal magic within them, and when they all worked together, the magic in them ensured both nature and humanity flourished. There were no famines, no pandemics, no war — it was pretty much as close to Utopia as it got. But as you'd expect, it was short lived. From what we've gathered, it seems like humans mucked it up pretty badly. They started wanting more concentrated amounts of power than what they were born with. People started killing each other as sacrifices and destroyed important resources to gain more individual power. Eventually, the universe took her gifts back. Instead, she fashioned children made in her image, and in them, she placed power that became uniquely theirs. That's how we were created. When you started appearing in our dreams, we knew another child of the universe had awakened. So, we watched you, waiting for a sign that you were ready. Each one of us started having dreams that helped in guiding us to one another. Though in your case, you just took off like a bat out of hell and instead of dreams, we kept getting pulled into your nightmares. We couldn't even try explaining anything to you since you just kept running away. It was different for all of us but after the dreams started, we all got sick. Every time one of us went through the experience, the others who had gone through it already were waiting to help. But we couldn't talk to you, so we had to keep watching. When we saw you were admitted with a fever, we knew it was time. We think you are a child of fire, blessed and burdened with the responsibility of protecting the element."

Sawyer remained silent, still refusing to believe that this was happening to her. What started as a giggle quickly morphed into hysterical laughter.

"Okay, okay, you guys had me in the 1st half, not gonna lie, but I give up. You win, Maddie!"

"Has she gone off her rocker?"

"Unbelievable."

The little hope Sawyer had that this was a prank started fading fast. Especially after neither Maddie nor anyone else jumped out. That meant that she was left to wonder if there was truth to what she was being told. At that moment, Sawyer decided she would have to get out of here no matter what the truth was. She was still vaguely listening to the ongoing conversation as she looked for a window. Some way, somehow, she would get out, but she couldn't escape if she didn't feel better. Sawyer would have to take the risk in assuming that these women were not actually trying to harm her. She opened the vial and swallowed the pink elixir.

3

Theres Always Karaoke

SAMANTHA

FUCK ME!

Her arm caught a piece of jagged metal protruding from the wall as she jumped over the side of the dumpster and slid behind it to hide herself. The blood dripped down her arm like lava against her wind-chilled skin. The pain of her open flesh stung like a paper cut on steroids. But the pain was good; it made her more alert and attentive.

On the other hand, tetanus I could do without.

She could hear the cars flying by each other a couple of streets away. In the building to her right, she could hear a male emcee on a microphone announcing that karaoke was about to start, which was met by the resounding cheer from the patrons of the bar. At the end of the alley, a collared cat screeched as it ran from a stray dog, both of them knocking over a bunch of discarded drink cans stacked on top of a rotting crate nearby.

Not the best hiding space, but a great vantage point at least.

She pressed herself into the wall, letting her head loll against the unpainted surface as she caught her breath. She might be able to find this funny later, but right now, her focus was on the five assholes who were currently after her. Sam glanced around, realizing that it was time to re-think her plan. She sighed, grimacing as she inhaled the stench of week-old, stale vomit — no doubt compliments of the bar. This was definitely not her best idea, but in retrospect, she'd had worse. Well, maybe not worse than this, and a quick mental scan over the last couple of years of her life proved that she couldn't produce anything that topped this. Nope, this was it: the disgusting alley, goons, stale trash, and old vomit. She was firmly sitting in the middle of rock bottom.

Sam smiled to herself and inspected her bleeding arm, tending to it under the flickering streetlight. She used her pocket knife to tear the hem of her favorite shirt and wrapped it around her arm to staunch the bleeding. The wound was deeper than she thought, something she only noticed as her blood automatically soaked through the makeshift bandage. She spun the small designer backpack around, unzipping it to glance at the diamond inside to make sure it was still safe.

Sawyer was being overloaded with information. Somewhere along the line, the conversation had gone down several tangents, and Sawyer was no longer sure what they were talking about anymore.

She was daydreaming when the elixir kicked in. All at once, her body stopped aching and the chills went away. She felt better than she had ever felt in her life. The others hadn't noticed her improved health, and she wasn't planning to say anything about it either. An hour later, and even with all the information being hurled at her, the most important thing on her mind was getting back home — especially now that she felt better. She didn't care that it was their medicine that had apparently saved her life.

Okay, Sawyer. Ask them for a bathroom and use the window to get out. Because who doesn't have a window in the bathroom, right?.

"Gotta watch she ya, she gine escape."

There's no *way.*

She wasn't sure if the shock she was feeling was also plastered all over her face. But what she did know was that she was now staring at Iyana whose body was half hidden by the refrigerator as she rummaged around inside.

"I'm not, I won't, *that's*—"

"Impossible. Yeah, we know. You've been saying." Amira snickered as she passed behind Sawyer.

Sawyer rolled her eyes at the chortle as Anabelle stared at them inquisitively. Iyana wasn't bothered at all as she continued digging around in the massive fridge.

Mind reading isn't possible; this isn't Twilight, for heaven's sake.

Maybe she'd been subconsciously whispering to herself and Iyana had somehow heard her. That, or because of her pure discomfort and apprehension, her body language had signaled a plan to escape. Had she been staring at the windows a little too long?

"I ain' even looking at you." The whisper was so close, the surprise of it made Sawyer spin around. There was no one there.

The anxiety in the pit of her stomach started to slowly morph into fear and panic, twisting itself together and making it harder to breathe as the seconds went by.

"Breeze before ya burn down de place. All you like you's do is freak out. Just relax."

The speed at which all the jumbled words flowed out of Iyana's mouth was enough to break Sawyer's resolve. She had no idea what Iyana had exactly said, but she understood the part about not freaking out. She was afraid and all alone with strangers. But as afraid as she was, she was also angry, and the more she thought about it, the angrier she got.

"What? I'm not, I couldn't possibly burn—"

Iyana cut her off before she could fall deeper into the pit of her denial. "Sweet girl, you listen to anything we was saying, 'cause it don' seem so?"

Iyana gave her an irritated glance, walking away, making the same frustrated sound as before.

Anabelle sent an understanding smile Sawyer's way before repositioning herself so she was closer to Sawyer. "Iyana can't read minds but, well, think of it this way. The sun's solar energy and magnetic fields affect every living thing on Earth, so Iyana has the ability to perceive deeply."

Even though Sawyer wasn't buying this, she still found herself listening intently as Anabelle continued.

"The mind magic was just a bit of telepathy, which — again — is related to how the sun has the ability to interact with everything. So, while she's not an empath, her magic is impressive and expansive." Anabelle paused to look off in the direction Iyana had gone before she whispered, "And she should be using it for better things than picking on you."

The ogre-in-charge tripped over some boxes as he and his merry band of idiots entered the alley. The stupid overhead street light was still flickering, making a less-than-ideal situation even worse than it already was. Her vision felt strained and compromised in the inconsistent lighting.

Okay….plan….Plan.

Plan for what?

For survival, because her choices were pretty simple — escape or get captured. She peeped at the approaching men from her dumpster hideaway. Twiddle Dee and Twiddle Dumb would be easier to handle if she took them out first, since they were at the front. She could see they were slow — the sweat stains on the armpits and necklines of their shirts, paired with the way they both hobbled along, let her know that they were also tired. They would be a piece of cake. That left her with the three behind them — the veiny-armed one who was still finding new ways to fall over himself, and the two following behind him looked like they had the mental capacity of an overripe banana. Five on one weren't great odds but they weren't the worst either, although Sam never underestimated the enemy; regardless of how educationally challenged they seemed.

If possible, she wanted to avoid close range combat — they were all bigger than she was and could inflict serious injury if they got their hands on her. In general, a fight could be fun, but dumb or not, with the right amount of force, a lucky strike from one of them could kill her.

She closed her eyes and breathed in the deepest, *calmest* breath she could manage without inhaling too much of the stench of her surroundings. She could hear the alley cats meowing, and the blaring horns from the traffic on the main street told her it hadn't slowed. The wind blew softly— she appreciated how it helped calm her nerves and pushed some of the putrid alley smells away from her face. She took another breath and — holding her hands out in front of her — materialized two solid spheres of ice. Sam glanced up at the approaching threat as the balls divided further — the one in her left hand into three smaller, perfectly shaped spheres, and the one in her right hand into two, all no bigger than the size of pennies. Sam transferred all of them into one hand, held it behind her back and, rolling her shoulders back so she could steady herself, she stepped out from behind the dumpster.

"Now, this game of hide and seek is tedious at best. I mean, I thought you would have found me by now." She shook her head at them, feigning disappointment.

"The diamond, Samantha. Hand it over!"

"Oh, would you look at that?! Giving me subject-verb agreement, and a full sentence with more than four words too! Good job." She flashed a smile at the head of the grizzly clan.

"Get the diamond. Kill her if you have to!"

So, she was right — they were as dumb as they appeared. That, or he hadn't *really* warned them of what she could do. Sam didn't even flinch at the threat.

"I'm sure *he* didn't give the order to kill me." She raised an eyebrow in question.

"So what? Accidents happen all the time and *you're* a pain in the ass. He knows *that*."

They started advancing towards her.

She closed her eyes and sent the previously concealed ice directly at the men approaching her. They froze as soon as the ice pellets hit them — their bodies encapsulated in solid glacial cocoons. Sam picked up her bag and, as she walked out of the alley swinging it, knocked over the last man closest to her, who shattered when he hit the ground.

"Whoops."

Sawyer paced back and forth in the room Anabelle had led her to a while ago, as she eavesdropped on the simmering argument taking place between the others.

"We have to let her go." Anabelle's voice was firm, like a good leader's would be, but so soft that Sawyer almost missed what she had said.

Sawyer had no confirmation, but from what she'd seen so far, Anabelle *had* to be in charge. She hoped. Since Anabelle was the only one pushing for her release.

"How you mean, leh she go?"

"Aye, she may be a wee melter but she needs to stay. She's one of us."

The responses came all at once, and the combination of accents and slang didn't make following along any easier.

She could hear that Anabelle was outnumbered but by some miracle, prayed the argument would end in her favour. She assumed Iyana and Amira would have been excited to kick her back into her old life. However, they had teamed up with Imogen and were trying to convince Anabelle of all the reasons why Sawyer needed to stay with them.

"We told her everything!" someone, it sounded like Amira, was yelling.

"And she doesn't want to be here. We can't force her, she'll—"

"Can't we, though?" Imogen was asking, having interrupted her sister.

"She'll come back when the time is right for her and—"

Iyana cut Anabelle off before she could finish. "Wait, you serious?" Iyana let out an exasperated groan. "So wuh was de point of grabbing she to begin wid? Wuh sorta shite is thi—"

"Iyana! We *will* let her go."

That was the loudest she had heard Anabelle's voice go since she was there. The silence was deafening as her words lingered in the air, and for a couple of minutes, the house felt devoid of life.

"Cool." She was curt in her dismissal, and Sawyer could hear her quiet footfall as she walked away.

Nothing else was said, but shortly after, the door to her room opened and someone walked in. Imogen looked at her from the doorway and with a sigh, she stepped to a side so Sawyer could pass — shoulders caved in like a disappointed 5-year-old's.

"You can leave." Imogen's face was somber.

Sawyer didn't know these women but she felt somewhat remorseful that she was causing so much tension. But she didn't feel guilty enough to consider staying.

"Thanks for whatever that pink stuff was." She forced a small smile as she walked towards the door.

"She means get out." Amira walked up and wrapped her right arm around Imogen's shoulders. "Now."

4

I'm Judging You Now

SAMANTHA

S AM WALKED AROUND TO the back of the building, climbed two stories up the fire escape and, glancing around to make sure no one was watching, pried open the window to an apartment. All the lights were off, so she carefully stuck her head inside to make sure no one was around. It was quiet tonight, the blissful kind of quiet that made the night instinctively more divine. The moon was full, and the sky was filled with clouds — the oversized, luscious ones that looked like marshmallows and not cirrus filaments. There weren't a lot of visible stars, but the ones she could see twinkled brightly. The soft breeze that made her hair dance around her face was cool and crisp. These were the kinds of nights she loved, and it had almost passed her by because she was in that shitty alleyway.

Trying to forget about the beginning of her night, she tucked her left leg through the window. With her right foot already on the ground, her left had barely touched the floor when a massive force slammed her against the wall, almost knocking the wind out of her.

This is what she'd been waiting for. Kaelan's hands on her body as he lifted her up and pinned her to the wall. Her legs automatically wrapped around him and she breathed in fiercely, smelling his skin before he kissed her. She'd missed him, but more than anything, she'd missed the smell of sunshine and burnt amber that always clung to his skin.

He was finally home.

"Ouch." Kaelan laughed as he pulled away from her and touched his lips.

"How long before you realized I wasn't a cat burglar?"

"I didn't think you were a burglar."

"Oh, you planned to have your secret girlfriend climb through our bedroom window then?" Sam wiggled her eyebrows and pushed down so he'd release her legs.

She took off her shirt, pulled her jeans down to her knees, and flopped down onto the bed. Laying face up, she pulled the hair-tie she usually wore on her hand, off her wrist. She used the last ounce of energy she had to put her untamed curls into a messy bun on the top of her head. Unable to wiggle out of her jeans any further, she exhaled gruffly in exasperation. Kaelan walked over chuckling, and pulled the pants off her legs before moving to flick on the overhead bedroom light.

"Thanks." Sam pulled her legs on to the bed and rolled over so she could watch him move around.

He unzipped one of his suitcases so he could unpack. Samantha propped her head on her right hand and smiled as he went.

"I missed you too, babe." He laughed as he stopped unpacking his suitcase midway. "I can definitely do this later."

He dimmed the light and made his way over to the bed. Sam was lying on her back with her head towards him and Kaelan rested on his side, looking into her eyes. His gaze scanned her body up and down before he took her arm into his hand.

"That looks like a nasty scratch, want to catch me up?" He motioned to the makeshift bandage.

"Oh yeah, that." She rolled off the bed to take care of the cut she had gotten earlier. Grabbing a towel, she made her way to the bathroom.

In three, two, one.

"Samantha! You got blood all over the bed!!"

She giggled stepping into the shower.

God, I'm glad he's home.

Slight cheering welcomed Sawyer as she walked through the doors of her sorority. She laughed when Maddie ran down the staircase, nearly tripping on the last two steps.

"Where were you? The hospital said you *left*. Just '*snuck out*'."

"Later." Sawyer didn't want to have the conversation in the middle of the foyer. She'd find a way to explain what happened to Maddie in private. She chuckled awkwardly, "I didn't sneak away though."

But she wanted to now — to slip off, straight to her room, before anyone started asking her questions she couldn't answer.

Sawyer finally saw an opening to slip away when they started talking about throwing a party to celebrate her recovery. She made her way up the stairs and got to her room, avoiding an interrogation. Sitting down on the bed, she pulled her knees to her chest, pressing the heels of her feet against the ledge of the bed frame to prop her legs up. Sawyer folded her arms across the top of her thighs and bent over, resting her forehead on her arms. Closing her eyes, she inhaled deeply.

It felt like years had passed, but barely any time had gone by since she went to the hospital and had been virtually kidnapped by the crazies. At least she was alone now, where she could enjoy the peace and quiet of her room. The door was locked to prevent Maddie from barging in to issue the third degree. She'd had enough bonding time and just needed some time alone. She let out a slow exhale.

Ten minutes later, Sawyer unfolded herself from the edge of the bed, walked over to the floor-length mirror so she could examine her reflection. She *looked* the same. She performed a tactile temperature check on herself in an attempt to locate her elevated temperature, but her fever was gone. She *felt* like the same person she was before she met them, *and* she felt like something inside her had changed.

She pulled the hair tie off her wrist and drew her hair into a messy bun at the top of her head, pushing the fly-aways behind her ears. She was tired—, no, she was *exhausted,* and even though she had finals to study for, she couldn't bring herself to open a textbook. So, instead of studying, she climbed into bed and curled herself into the fetal position. Just five minutes, maybe ten, and then she'd be ready to jump headfirst back into assignments and term papers like nothing had changed. A tear slid down her cheek as she drifted off to sleep.

It was still dark outside when she woke up, but there were no stars in the sky. She rolled over and looked at the clock confirming that she'd definitely slept too long. Her five-minute nap had turned into five hours; so, if Maddie had tried to get in, Sawyer didn't hear her. She peeked over the edge of the bed, eyeing a piece of paper on the floor. Begrudgingly, she got out of bed and retrieved it. Sawyer unlocked the door and reached for her phone so she could message Maddie.

Sawyer was wide awake now, which meant she could cram for a while before she had to go to class. Reaching for her bag she pulled out her Fundamental Principles of Microbiology, rolled over onto her back again and closed her eyes as she rested the heavy book on her abdomen. Fifteen minutes later, she repositioned herself onto her stomach and finally started flipping through the pages of the book. The words eventually started blurring together as she passively read while her mind drifted back to the women from earlier — page after page, word after word and all she could think about was what they had told her, what she saw Amira do and what they said *she* would be able to do one day.

The thoughts kept coming and the more she thought of them, the further she spiraled, absolutely fixated on the day's events. Sawyer let out an audible gasp as she realized that she hadn't had a dream tonight. She looked at the clock. It was five a.m. now. She'd slept through the night. A moment of elation hit her; she had finally gotten her first good night's rest in what had felt like months. Ecstatic, she danced in bed, smiling as she let out a tension-releasing sigh. Reading the last few pages of the current chapter, Sawyer put down her book, closed her eyes, and snuggled back into her bed. Fingers crossed she'd be awake with enough time to get ready for class before it started.

Sam looked over at Kaelan and smiled. She thought there was something so enchanting about just watching him sleep — the way his breaths were light and soft as he rustled around under the sheets. She glanced through the window, looking at the moon, and smiled once more as she thought about how she would spend the day doing absolutely nothing, with the love of her life. She snuggled her body up close to him and wiggled her feet until they were nestled in between his. She glanced up at him from her new position and then closed her eyes, letting herself relax. Eventually, her breathing began to match his until she lost all consciousness and drifted off into a heavy slumber.

Samantha watched as she ran through a forest, three girls chasing her. She'd only glanced back about twice the entire time. The girls had lost her when she feinted left and ran through a bunch of trees on the right instead. They stopped to regroup and she was able to run uninterrupted. She was traveling at full speed when she hit a twisted branch and tumbled over. She watched herself get up, dust her clothes off and squint through the forest's twisted shadows before she took off into a run again.

Sam flew up into a seated position like someone had slapped her awake. Her breathing was shallow and heavy as she unconsciously stared into the shadows of their bedroom. In the distance, she could hear Kaelan faintly calling her name but her response felt like molasses in her mouth. He placed a soft kiss on her temple, dropping his forehead to rest on her shoulder.

"Sammy?"

She tilted her head towards him slightly.

"Please, come back to me."

After a few minutes, Sam started slowly reacting to the sound of Kaelan's voice, and her breathing began to slow and soften. She focused on the longing in his voice and the image behind her eyes started to dematerialize. It was her — different, but her. She looked directly into her own eyes but couldn't recognize herself.

Don't think about them. Don't think about it. It doesn't have anything to do with your stupid dream.

Memories that she had tried to forget flashed to the forefront of her mind. Her life in foster care before being adopted. Her wonderful adoptive parents taking her home — those parents being stolen from her and the prison she'd grown up in afterward. The isolation. She'd been privately tutored, and when she wasn't focused on academia, she was in combat and weapons training. Her 11th birthday gift had been a JNG-90, not a birthday party. And although she could speak a plethora of languages by that age, she had no one to talk to.

She tried hard to push away the feelings of anger, resentment, and grief, burying them as deep as they would go. But they swirled around together in her chest. Her parents were amazing, and their love for her had cost them their lives. The need for vengeance reared its ugly head from the deepest part of her soul.

"Samantha," his voice was close to a whimper as he began to shake her out of her stupor. His desperation breaking through the fog.

Sam looked down at Kaelan's leg and his irritated skin outlining her freezing fingertips. He hadn't made a sound of discomfort, even though she knew her hand was causing him pain. She slowly removed her fingertips from his skin and leaned over to kiss the spots she'd unintentionally created.

"It's okay. *I'm* okay." Kaelan tenderly shifted her position so he could hold her chin in his hand and look her in the eyes. "Hey, where'd you go?"

Kaelan was waiting for her answer when she shamefully dropped her gaze from his. He leaned into her and placed a gentle kiss on her lips, and she knew it was because he was fully aware that only one thing made her upset enough for her to lose the ability to control her magic.

"I promise I'm alright," he reiterated, before she could ask for the second time.

"Sorry." She was looking at his thigh again. Her fingers tracing the first-degree frostbite marks her trauma plunge had left on his skin.

"Come here." Kaelan pulled her into him, placing a gentle kiss on her forehead.

"You have half an hour left."

The professor continued talking, but Sawyer wasn't paying attention to what was being said.

She was too busy daydreaming — a welcome break from the ongoing nightmares. Sawyer adjusted her head so that it rested comfortably in the palm of her hand as she propped her elbow on the desk she was sitting at.

He was attractive, and muscular in places she didn't know muscles could exist. He had a deep dimple on his left cheek and the purest smile she had ever seen. And when he kissed her as he pinned her to the bed, the way his dark hazel eyes sparkled, made her shiver. If the perfect man existed, Sawyer was a hundred percent sure that this was him.

"Twenty minutes left." She shook her head and smiled, realizing she had wasted another ten minutes. She filled in the rest of the test sheet as quickly as she could and turned the paper in.

"You didn't need to show up, Ms. Elias, you already have an A." He took the paper and placed it in the submission bin.

"But that's not an A plus, professor," she whispered before heading out through the door, his chuckle following her out.

Sawyer walked to her car, thoughts of a hot shower dominating her mind. She still didn't want to deal with, or talk to, anyone. What she wanted were her snacks and trinkets on one side of her bed, and her laptop on the other, so she could catch up on shows. She was stressed, but as she threw her bag in the passenger seat, she couldn't help but smile to herself — at least her finals were over.

Pulling out of the parking lot, she saw a flash of blue hair in her peripheral vision and, for a split second, her anxiety flared. She forcefully hit the breaks, jolting the car to an abrupt stop — her palms sweaty, and her heart rate accelerated. She looked around but there was no one there. She shook her head in an attempt to shake off the unease.

I'm just exhausted. Imogen isn't following me. No one's watching me.

Sawyer eased her foot off the break paddle and drove away.

5

This Math Thing

SAWYER BYPASSED A GROUP of her sorority sisters who were making cleaning schedules and other party prep lists. She hadn't been able to figure out why they were still so insistent on throwing her a party, but ultimately decided that what they needed was any reason to party so why waste her time trying to fight them on it? She already planned to just hide out in her room anyway.

She got into the shower and, despite the stress from everything that had happened, she realized that today felt great. No one had kidnapped her, and that was the bare minimum for a good day but she counted it as a win. The warm water from the shower hit the top of her head and instantly relaxed her. For a moment, she watched the old silk press fade away, replaced by bouncy curls that stretched out the wetter they got. Running her hand from her forehead to the nape of her neck, she tried to recall the daydream from earlier that day.

After her shower, Sawyer put on pajamas and nestled herself into bed — curtains drawn, shows ready, world off. Four episodes in and she could feel the sleep she had been fighting earlier gradually creeping up on her, dialogues slurring into indistinct murmuring. Her thoughts started drifting off to the imaginary man from before — his smile bouncing around in her mind. The voices outside her door sounded like they were miles away. She was fighting to keep her eyes open but she'd spent all her energy suppressing her emotional fatigue. Now it felt too heavy to bear, so, she stopped fighting it and blissfully slipped into sleep's warm embrace.

She was pressed against a bedpost in a room with an industrial interior and tasteful decor. The room and all its furnishings were minimal and elegant, all except the bed. It took up most of the room, and the intricate corners of the canopy posts made the already large bed seem larger. The mattress was covered in way too many pillows for her taste, but there was so much space that it didn't seem to matter in the exquisitely plush wonderland of the bed.

Sawyer could feel his muscular hands around her wrists as he held her hands above her head. She heard herself giggle as she looked lovingly up at the man with a dreamy pair of bedroom eyes. He laughed in response to her actions as she squirmed to get free from his hold.

His laugh was deep and rich; it echoed in her head like the acoustics of a cathedral, making her dizzy. She watched as she pulled him closer and kissed him passionately, like she couldn't get close enough to him no matter how much she deepened the kiss. They moved together, in a wordless embrace — their movement in sync as they kissed and groped each other, moving on to the bed. Laughs and giggles filled the air as they playfully fought each other to gain control . When she finally forced him to roll over, she used her legs to pin him to the bed.

"Gotcha!" she said, before planting a quick kiss on his cheek.

He smiled up at her beautifully, his single dimple deepening, and pulled her forward, kissing her and running his hands underneath her shirt.

Sawyer wanted to watch more — this was the best dream she'd had in months — but the images started to fade as she moved his hands, adjusting her shirt as she ran her eyes down the length of his body. The last thing she saw was herself moving into a sitting position on top of him so that she could tie her hair up into a ponytail. Their gazes were locked and he smirked as she started to shimmy herself lower down his body.

Stay asleep. Don't you dare wake up.

But the harder she tried, the more Sawyer could feel her dream melting away.

Kaelan kissed her softly on the nose before he rolled off her and sprawled his large body across his side of the bed. She glanced over at his goofy smile before she got up to take a shower, watching as he reached for the sheet to cover his lower body.

"You're no fun at all." She playfully wagged her finger at him.

"Weren't you going to shower?" He was laughing as he closed his eyes. "I'm not going to sleep, by the way. So, keep talking if you want."

She shook her head as she walked into the bathroom and turned on the water, looking at herself in the mirror.

"Did you leave the TV on?" Sam leaned out through the bathroom door.

Kaelan opened his eyes and she could see the confusion spread across his face.

"What?"

"The TV. Something was playing a minute ago."

"Playing where?"

"Go check to see if it's on." She leaned back into the bathroom.

Sam heard Kaelan groan, then followed the sound of his footsteps as he walked into the living room.

He popped his head into the bathroom a few minutes later. "There's nothing on, like I told you. Do I need to be worried or did you take something?" He chuckled.

She was completely sober. So maybe her mind was playing tricks on her — first with the flashbacks and now with the TV hallucination. She was sure she could hear a song playing softly, accompanied by a muffled conversation a little while ago. Or maybe her sleep deprivation was finally making her lose her mind.

"Eh, forget it. You coming to shower?"

"In a bit."

Samantha stepped into the shower, allowing the running hot water to soothe her. She stood as it soaked her hair and ran down her body, closing her eyes to relish the feeling of the scalding water against her skin. She'd been standing there for a while after she had actually finished showering, hoping the water would wash her thoughts away, when she felt Kaelan's presence behind her.

She turned around and looked at him. In his eyes, she could see that he knew she'd got lost in her thoughts again. She knew he just wanted her to be okay, and she hated seeing the sadness and frustration on his face because he knew he couldn't take her pain away. Sam fought the unbearable feelings of sadness she would sometimes get, gathered them together, and pushed them into her box of repressed feelings. Taking his face in her hands, she pressed a soft kiss to his lips before turning to face the shower so the water could run down her face.

Kaelan hugged her as the water, she knew was too hot for his skin, hit his hands and arms. He flinched a little and she reached for the shower handle to lower the temperature.

"Better?" She glanced behind her to smile at him.

"Much better." He planted a kiss into the crook of her neck as he tightened his arms around her.

They stood there in silence for a while — the only sound, the water from the shower as it slapped against the tiles and glass. He was the only person to see her drop her guard, but even then, it usually happened when she thought she was alone. Sam hated feeling vulnerable and forlorn. It was an uncomfortable departure from her usual confidence.

"Even when you're sad, you're still the most breathtaking woman I've ever seen," he whispered into her ear.

She felt her smile soften and she turned around to face him, pressing her bare breasts against his chest so she could hug him back. She loved how much he treasured her — how he would do whatever he could to make her happy — so she held onto him with everything she had.

After about five minutes of being in his arms Sam lightly kissed Kaelan and got out of the shower, leaving him so he could get clean. Walking back into the bedroom, she smiled as she realized he had pulled the blackout curtains closed to eliminate any light. He'd also plugged out all their electronics and put clean sheets on the bed . She really did miss him when he was gone. She walked over to the dresser so she could take one of his t-shirts from a drawer. She shimmied into some underwear, threw his shirt on, and snuggled back into bed.

The sound of her phone ringing obnoxiously woke her up. It was ringing — not buzzing against the surface of the side table — which meant that it was Kaelan. Through her blurry vision, she peeped over her shoulder for confirmation that he was gone. She reached for her phone, but before she could answer it, the ringtone cut off. She double-tapped the screen and saw that she'd missed eight calls from Kaelan.

What the hell?!

Sam hit the redial button and when he didn't answer on the first ring, her worry began taking root, growing expeditiously with every ring until he finally picked up.

"Are you okay?"

"I'm fine, but you need to get up and get packed because I was *supposed* to be gone 30 minutes ago."

Sam looked around the room and saw piles of her clothes stacked on the edge of the bed, along with two suitcases in the middle of the room.

"I'm coming this time?!"

She couldn't hide the excitement in her voice at the thought of travelling with him. Something they hardly ever got a chance to do because their schedules never aligned.

"Not if you don't hurry up and get down here."

"Okay, okay, packing! I'll be there in twenty minutes."

"No, you won't," he laughed before hanging up the phone.

He was right. Although she could probably make it to the airport in ten minutes, it would take her thirty minutes minimum to pack, especially if she was going to go through all the clothes he'd dumped out on the bed. The alternative was throwing a whole bunch of stuff into the suitcases and figuring it out when she got there. Speed, not efficiency, was her chosen plan of attack.

When she opened the bag prepared to throw the first pile of her clothes inside, neatly packed in the top right corner, were a couple sets of her lingerie — all Kaelan's favourites. She laughed as she tossed the clothes in, reaching for the second pile.

Of course.

Twenty-five minutes later she walked towards him, smiling, as he glanced down at his watch. She was confident — she'd checked the time she took to get there after she got out of the car.

"I'm ready, let's go."

Kaelan stepped aside and pointed her towards the jet. "After you."

Sam hesitated before taking the first step. "Wait, where are we going?"

"Just go, Sammy. I'll fill you in later. We're late."

Sawyer rolled around in her bed and stretched out for an extended moment before she slid off and decided to go to the kitchen. Thoughts of the dream still floated around in her head — she was annoyed that she'd woken up before the really good parts.

The Sorority was quiet tonight. All the planning for "her" welcome home party had come to a halt. Some of the girls had decided to go out, a few had already gone to bed, and others were studying to wrap up finals.

There were groups of girls spread out between heaps of books all over the main rooms of the house; a couple of the groups were straight up sleeping. She sighed, soaking in her appreciation for the quiet time. Walking into the kitchen, she made herself a cup of instant coffee and sat down on one of the stools by the island.

Finishing off her cup, she washed it and started heading back to her room when she was stopped by one of the few girls who was still awake.

"Um, Kat sent me to you. I needed help with this math thing. I know it's pretty late, but I was studying when I noticed you walk into the kitchen, and thought I should take my chance to ask now. I hope you don't mind?"

Sawyer had to stop herself from smiling at how obviously nervous the girl was. She hadn't talked to a lot of the newer girls in the sorority — for no particular reason really, if she were to think of it.

She felt kind of shitty that she hadn't taken the time to get to know them, especially since almost all of them seemed to know her. She'd make up for it once her life settled down a bit, but helping this freshman seemed like a good first step.

"Yeah sure, no problem. I'm pretty free since I'm done with finals anyways. Give me a couple of minutes."

Sawyer ran upstairs to her room, grabbed her books, and started making her way back downstairs when she stopped walking mid-stairs.

"This is your captain speaking, I would like to thank you for flying with us. We are about to land so fasten your seat belts — we'll be landing in five minutes."

She jumped at the sound in her head.

What the fuck is going on?

She could see the girl looking at her, confused by her sudden pause as she lingered in the middle of the staircase.

"Are you okay? I mean we can do this later if you're still sick." The girl had taken a few steps closer and was now standing with her foot on the bottom step.

"No, I'm fine." She smiled at the girl to offer some reassurance, quickly walking towards her.

But deep down, she felt like something was wrong with her. Maybe she was being paranoid, but she felt pretty certain that whatever was happening had something to do with the mysterious pink elixir she'd accepted from a bunch of strangers.

6

Stupidity or Insanity?

SAMANTHA

Samantha was in the backseat of the town car, watching the raindrops cling to the windows for a nanosecond before they were blown away and replaced by new ones. The rain provided the perfect accompaniment to her reverie, and Kaelan, who had fallen asleep in her lap, wasn't a bad addition either.

The scenery was gorgeous; breathtakingly so. There were evergreen trees everywhere, and she found the gloomy environment to be quite charming. She was at ease, captivated by the simple splendor of nature. It was strange but it felt like home.

Sam couldn't tell whether the feelings she had were coming from the fact that she was in a place of indescribable beauty, or if they were merely a consequence of being with Kaelan. Glancing down at him, she smiled at how the silhouettes from the scenery beyond the car window painted murals across his face as they drove.

The shadows of the raindrops danced on his skin and, every once in a while, the different kinds of lights refracting through the water created mini rainbows that stood out against his lighter complexion.

When they finally reached the hotel, she nudged him awake. Thankfully he didn't wake up groggy and grumpy, like she would have. It didn't take long for them to check-in, and she inspected their opulent hotel room while they waited for their bags to be sent up.

"Want to order room service?" Kaelan was undressing, looking out the window at the evergreens.

"Sure. I didn't realize how hungry I was 'til just now. Let me look—"

A knock at the door announcing the arrival of their bags interrupted the conversation. By the time the hotel porter had delivered their bags inside, Sam had already ordered them more food than they would eat.

"Being able to order room service on the TV screen with just a couple of clicks? It's a brilliant thing."

Kaelan shook his head and started rummaging through his bag, determined to pull some of his clothes and all of his toiletries out before the food got there. Samantha watched as he organized his stuff, then he started working on hers.

"No wonder you got to the airport so fast, you just threw in everything," he laughed as he finished unpacking.

"Laugh all you want; it was an intelligent strategy." She disrobed and climbed into bed while Kaelan put some of her clothes in the closet.

After dragging their empty bags into a corner, Kaelan climbed into bed behind her. They nestled together and waited for their food, while he traced small circles on her stomach. Sam was enjoying the moment but couldn't shake the feeling that something was different. She couldn't tell if the change was a bad one or something good, but whatever it was, felt a tad unsettling.

Sawyer hadn't got enough sleep when her alarm went off. She'd forgotten to disable it after spending the rest of the night helping Taylor, the freshman who played volleyball.

"Turn it off." Maddie's muffled grumbling was barely audible from the other side of the room.

Sawyer reached out towards her side table without opening her eyes and tapped around until she felt the glass surface under her fingers. Squinting at the bright light from her phone screen, she slid the arrow and hit snooze.

"Finally," another muffled grumble came from Maddie.

Sawyer groaned in response, refusing to speak, convinced that maintaining the silence might help her get back to sleep. She thought back to what she'd experienced on the staircase. It would be naive of her to think that it had nothing to do with drinking the strange liquid. But was she going to start believing in magic? Sawyer wasn't sure if she was ready to open that can of worms.

I can't ignore what I saw Amira do.

Did I actually see it though, or was it the fever? A fever that mysteriously disappeared when I drank whatever was in that vial.

She didn't like the fact that the only two explanations appeared to be: being stupid enough to doubt her own experience — questioning what she'd seen with her own two eyes. Or, being insane enough to believe a bunch of strangers, who kidnapped her to tell her magic was real.

Sawyer didn't have time to think about it, or rather — if she was being honest — she didn't want to think about it. But she needed to know more and should have paid attention to what Amira and the others were explaining to her.

On the bright side, she now had a lot of time on her hands, thanks to the semester winding down. She decided to use her time and reach out to Imogen — maybe they'd still be willing to help her, even after she'd panicked and left.

Unless none of this is real and I've lost my mind.

She spent the next twenty-five minutes trying to go back to sleep, and after the latest failed attempt, she finally got out of bed. Maddie was still asleep so she left the blinds closed and committed to stumbling around in the dark, looking for everything she needed to get showered; she would dress in the bathroom.

After enjoying berry waffles and coffee in the breakfast nook, she returned to her room, thoroughly enjoying her first day of no exams. Maddie was sitting on the bed in an ocean of open textbooks.

"When's your last final?" she asked, peering over the top of her glasses.

"I'm done. The last one got pushed up to yesterday." Sawyer flopped down on their small, shared sofa.

"I'm so jealous, I could vomit." Maddie pushed her glasses up and started reading again.

Sawyer started gathering her textbooks from the semester, so she could get the jump on returning them. Once everything was stacked in organizational piles, she walked over and sat on the window sill near her bed. From there, she could see directly into the courtyard of the sorority house — the outside world was finally starting to wake up and she would enjoy watching it for a while.

"I've got a couple errands to run today."

What she heard instead was 'you can do whatever you want today cause I'll be busy' and she was okay with that. Although she did want to spend every minute of the day with him, she wouldn't refuse the chance to explore the hotel while he worked. If he didn't ask her to go with him, she wouldn't make a big deal out of it. She had already planned to check out the hotel's spa anyway.

"But you can come with me if you want," he continued, shrugging like it didn't matter before flashing a smile as he waited for her answer.

"How nice, an invitation. But first, I have to decide if what you're doing is worth more to me than spending the entire day in pajamas." Sam stuck out her tongue before smirking.

"Can I take that as a yes?" Kaelan was chuckling at her antics.

"Take it as whatever you want, it's not a yes until I know what you're doing."

"I'm supposed to be looking for a rare book. According to my boss, this 'especially important piece of history' is located in a library somewhere here." He gestured around at nowhere in particular.

She raised an eyebrow at him.

"At least she thinks it is." Kaelan plopped down on the edge of the bed, rolling his eyes.

"Maybe you can walk around— converse with some students while I walk the aisles of the university's library? Fingers crossed that this doesn't take the entire day, or that I can rule out this location first and start looking somewhere else. You could make a friend." He melodiously stretched the d at the end of the word friend.

Sam whined unintelligibly, not willing to encourage Kaelan in his misguided hope that she might want to hang out with a university student for fun. She didn't want friends— least of all friends she probably had nothing in common with, and she would bet her bottom dollar that there wasn't much she had in common with co-eds.

"But you're my friend, isn't that enough?" She hopped out of bed with a small sigh and walked over to the closet.

Forty-five minutes later, she was taking in all the scenery the university had to offer as they pulled up to a parking space. Kaelan was talking to her and she wasn't paying much attention to him or anything he was saying. She snapped back to reality when he turned off the car and started opening his door. He must have seen the glazed-over look in her eyes, and the confusion stamped across her face, because he chuckled and repeated what he told her a minute earlier.

"I said, I might be gone for hours so you can come inside with me if you want, and maybe read a book. Talk to a librarian. Help me?" He laughed as he got out of the car, adding activities to her to-do list. He closed the door and leaned on the side, pushing his head through the driver-side window so he could point out what he was talking about.

"That's the building over there," He motioned toward a huge building with a red roof that peaked out from behind two smaller structures. "But in case you forget, I texted you a picture. I might not have service inside if you get lost." He paused for a second, turning to look her in the eye. "This is your last chance to tag along."

"Nah, I'm good. I'll probably just chill here. I still have episodes downloaded on my phone I can catch up on. I'll text you if I decide to get out and explore though." Sam sweetly smiled back at him.

"Suit yourself. See you in a bit."

Samantha watched him walk until he disappeared. She rolled her window down and reclined her seat a little, dangling her feet through the window and opening a pack of gummy bears she'd stashed in her bag. Perfect location for people-watching for the time being, but she knew Kaelan was right— she would get bored eventually and probably end up walking around, especially if he didn't find that book soon.

I really hope the return line at the library isn't too long.
I should have gotten more eBooks.

Sawyer dragged open the solid wooden door to the library, immediately scanning the room so she could locate the tail-end of the snaked line, made up of students all waiting to return their text-books. She'd seen worse lines and that's why she'd shown up so early. The line was wrapped around a couple times already, and the main entrance to the doorway would soon be completely blocked. The next ten to fifteen people would definitely send the line through the door of the building.

Sawyer thought back to her freshman year when she decided that dropping off her books later in the day was the ideal approach to take. Quickly, she learned the error of her mistake because nothing about late day returns was ideal. She'd ended up being stuck in the cold outside for an *hour* before she'd even gotten close to the library door. Being stuck at the library door was the worst part — people were constantly coming in and out of the library which meant that you were either in their way when they were trying to enter and ended up opening the door for them. Or you were in their way when they were trying to leave the library so you might get hit by the door when they pushed it open. When she had finally returned her books, her arms were sore from constantly opening the door and shielding her face from being smacked by it. The entire process had wasted several hours of her life. Never again.

I just want to get this done so that I can figure out what's going on with this apparent quasi-schiz-ophrenic episode. I really hope this isn't a side effect of tincture to lure me back in so I have to ask for a cure.

She took a couple steps forward as she continued her internal monologue, and by the time she had stopped complaining to herself about how awkward it would be to ask these girls for help, after she had told them all to shove it, she was at the front of the line.

Thankfully, she was among her type of people, so naturally, everyone had all their books and return slips ready. The actual process would only take her around ten minutes — a drastic im-provement from the previous three-hour experi-ence. When she was done, she pushed the ma-hogany doors open and inhaled a crisp gust of air, elated to be done with school for some time. The sun shone a little brighter and the birds sang a little happier, and Sawyer laughed out loud because, for the first time in a while, so was she.

"Sammy! Sam!"

Sawyer looked around instinctively to see who was screaming across the quad, but she couldn't figure out where the voice was coming from, so she turned and continued walking. They weren't talking to her anyway, so she should stop being nosy.

"Oh, come on, Sam, silent treatment because I wanted you to make friends with the librarian?" A rich laugh followed the question.

The voice was closer to her now — the sound of feet hitting the pavement let her know that the person had started to jog a little, probably hoping to catch up to whoever he was talking to. She didn't turn around to look, but she could still hear the laughter in his voice as he called after Sam, and when he chuckled, it made her laugh too. His laugh. Sawyer came to a dead stop at the realization that this, the sound of perfect laughter that she was hearing now, was the same as her dream. She swung around just as he started jogging to catch up to "Sam", and they collided. Her mouth dropped open as she stared into the vaguely familiar hazel eyes.

Of course, you had a dream about a man you'd seen on campus. Probably saw him with whoever Sam is too.

"Oh sorry, I thought you were—" he stopped before he could finish his sentence and ran a hand down his face. "You look; you look exactly like her. No, this is insane. I was about to ask if you beat up someone and stole their clothes." He laughed to try to hide his embarrassment at mistaking her for his friend.

Sawyer stared at him awkwardly.

Stop being an awkward idiot. You definitely saw him somewhere before and started dreaming about him. Just because you've never officially met someone doesn't mean that you can't dream about them. Say something.

Sawyer still hadn't said anything.

"Would you mind waiting here for a minute, or letting me get a picture of you? My girlfriend will never believe me if I just tell her." He smiled and his dimples almost swallowed her whole. She blinked to focus.

"Um, sorry but I'm late for something. And I don't let strange men take pictures of me no matter how adorably they might ask." She started walking off before he could respond.

He'd started to follow her. "No problem. The picture thing makes a lot of sense actually. But I promise it will take a second for me to grab her then."

He was next to her now, having used his larger strides to catch up— hands clasped together as he silently mouthed the word please, begging her to wait.

The interaction was bizarre and she was beginning to feel frantic. Like a house cat who'd been backed into a corner by an aggressively erratic child trying to pick it up. Sawyer laughed softly and agreed, though she *knew* he had no girlfriend and hoped this was a bad attempt at trying to pick her up and not a ruse where she could get kidnapped, *again.*

"Sure, you can grab her. I'll wait here."

"Thank you!" He turned on his heels and headed in the direction of the parking lot to the right of where they were standing.

As soon as she was sure he wouldn't glance behind him again, she picked up the pace and started briskly walking in the opposite direction.

7
Ready or Not

SAMANTHA

SAM HAD GOTTEN OUT of the car a playlist later, which also happened to be the same time she ran out of her snack. She put on her sweatshirt over the ribbed camisole she was wearing and locked the car, convincing herself that a walk through the campus was just what the doctor ordered. She was going for the scenery and fresh air, but her first priority was locating a place where she could buy some much needed coffee.

She'd been walking for five minutes and there was still no coffee shop in sight, but on her little adventure, she'd flipped off approximately eight random people who just wouldn't stop staring at her. Sam had made up her mind to walk up to the next person who rudely gawked at her and ask them for the location of an on-campus coffee shop. But as she rounded a corner, she found herself smack dab in the middle of a street filled with a litany of shops and bookstores. She smelled the coffee before she even saw the *"Cafe and a Cuppa"* sign. Fifteen minutes later, she was making her way through the bustling avenue with a white chocolate mocha and a cream cheese muffin topped with toasted pistachios.

Equipped with her caffeine and pastry, Sam roamed down the cobblestone lane back the way she'd come and made sure to stay clear of the library so she wouldn't be tempted to interrupt Kaelan. He could continue looking for his important book in peace. She could explore a little while longer, now that she had the building in sight and knew she wasn't lost.

It'd been just under two hours since she had started walking around, and not only had it been quite a trek to locate the coffee, but she was getting worn-out at random people making awkward faces at her clothes. Besides the sugary goodness and nice crisp air, so far walking around hadn't been as relaxing as she'd hoped for. It was mostly ignoring annoying stares and the occasional individual getting exasperated when they waved at her and she didn't wave back.

Time to go back to the car. It's too early to deal with this shit.

Sam made her way down some steps that led her to a huge quad paved with purple bricks and a peculiar sculpture in the middle. She had to give it to whoever built this campus; it was nice as hell. For a split second, she paused her trek, and imagined taking classes here, but then quickly resumed walking until she was kitty-corner from where she'd started the hunt for her coffee.

She stopped and sat down on a bench situated at the top of a little incline, but near enough to the quad and parking lot that she could see the car if she looked for it. It was completely shaded, sitting directly under a giant cherry tree. The tree was in full bloom and the light pink blossoms were radiant. The path didn't seem to have a lot of foot traffic, and maybe that was the reason she felt a wave of calm when she sat down. If Kaelan needed her, he would call. He couldn't get himself into much trouble looking for a book, and clearly he wasn't back at the car yet since he hadn't called.

Sam tucked her legs under her and pulled the hood of her sweatshirt up. Then, pushing her earbuds in and turning the music up to deafening levels, she relaxed onto the bench, biting into the still warm muffin.

Worth it.

Kaelan couldn't believe his eyes when he ran up to a complete stranger thinking she was Sam. It didn't take him too long to notice the faux pas but he was already jogging towards her confused face by then. Sam would never believe him, so he was glad the woman had agreed to stay for at least a couple minutes while he ran to get her.

He headed across the quad of purple bricks, cutting across a piece of lawn with a "stay off the grass" sign, so he could make it back to the parking spot in record time. He had just gotten to the top of the small hill when he looked back and saw the lookalike making a beeline for the street. He didn't move, but watched her to see where she was going instead.

I know this is probably creepy but I need her and Sam to meet.

He hoped the two of them would be so caught up with the fact that they looked exactly alike, that him temporarily losing his sanity and quasi-stalking the mystery lady to make the meeting happen wouldn't come up in conversation. And luckily for him, the woman didn't go far. From his vantage point on top of the small hill, he saw her

take a right and turn on to Sorority Row. Thankfully, she was wearing a coat bright enough for him to
track her movements through all the other bobbing
heads. There was no need to run to the car now —
he knew exactly where to search for her. Turning
back, he continued at a much more leisurely pace,
traipsing back to the car to grab Sam. His ringing
phone broke his focus.

"Babe!"

"Don't 'babe' me — are you soon done?"

"Sam! Yes! I'm heading back to the car now.
I need to show you something!"

"Good, 'cause I'm bored and it's been almost *three hours* since you went looking for that
thing. I'm not in the car but I'll start coming back
now. You better hope whatever you have to show
me is nicer than a cherry blossom tree or some
purple bricks."

"Samantha, where are you?" He told himself he needed to be a lot calmer and a lot steadier
to elicit her participation. But the excitement was
so great, he was holding his breath in anticipation
of her response.

"I told you; I'm walking towards the car
now. Stop being strange and just meet me there."

"Forget the car! If you're in or near the
purple quad, I can't see you. Are you—? You must

be at the other end. Walk until you see the white benches under the sequoia, then make a left and come towards the hill near the parking lot."

"What? I'm off to the side, but I'm already walking towards the parking lot. Do you see the Cherry tree on that small incline?"

Kaelan spun around, his eyes scanning every direction, hoping to see where Sam was coming from. Eventually, he spotted the tree off in the distance, to the right of the parking lot.

"I'll be there in maybe two—"

Kaelan didn't mean to but he hung up on her.

He stared at the screen wondering if she would call him again. He tried calling her back but she didn't pick up, and after a couple minutes passed, he spotted her walking towards him. When Samantha finally got there, he couldn't tell if she was more bewildered or exasperated by his behaviour. He jogged to meet her and they walked back to the car together.

"Nice of you to accompany me since you hung up the phone."

"I didn't mean to, I—,"

"Yeah, yeah," Samantha cut him off. "Now what do you *need* me to see? I'm hungry."

She made it back to her room after triple-checking she hadn't been followed. Screw waiting for New Year's resolutions— she needed a change and it was going to happen *immediately* because everything in her life felt insane. She looked around the room, glad that she was alone. Sawyer threw herself across her bed, hitting it like a bag of potatoes. Reaching for the phone and already regretting her decision, she scrolled through her messages. She located the "in case you change your mind" text from the unsaved number and hit the call button.

Sawyer sat on her bed, listening to the phone ring. Once. Twice.

Oh God, please *God let this be Imogen's phone.*

The phone kept ringing and her stomach sank with every ring.

No one's answering. Just hang up.

"Imogen speaking!"

Thank goodness.

"Hey, Imogen. This is Sawyer, I don't know if you remember me but—"

"Of course, I remember who you are. You alright?"

The friendly way Imogen talked to Sawyer made her feel even worse about the way she left, especially now that she was calling to ask for help.

"I was wondering if you could help me wi—"

"Immy, who you talking to? I was hollering fuh you fuh like thirty minutes girlie. "

There was no mistaking who that was. She could hear Iyana's thick accent even through the phone. She waited for Imogen to answer, hoping that she wouldn't tell Iyana who was on the line. Sawyer knew that her chances for help would decrease significantly if she found out. Honestly, she would probably not get help at all.

"Blimey Iyana! Have a day off, why don't ya? I heard you screaming my name in the most detestable way about three times after I told you I was coming."

There was a brief moment of silence that echoed through on Sawyer's end of the line.

"Wait lemme lef you boa. Ga long pon de phone. Just don't fuhge—"

"To come to you when I'm done. I know, I know."

There was another pause before Imogen redirected her voice back into the mouthpiece of the receiver.

"Love her to bits but Iyana can be a little gobby sometimes, innit?" Imogen giggled. "But never mind her, were you saying you needed help?"

"Yeah, I do. I think I'm losing my mind."

Imogen's melodic laughter lit up the phone line, baffling Sawyer who was being the most serious she had ever been in her life.

"Now, besides meeting us lot, why would you be losing your mind?"

"*Because* I had a dream about a guy and then I *met* him today!"

"Sounds more like luck than anything else if you ask me, love."

"You're not understanding me. At first, I thought I might have seen him somewhere, or with someone, but the more I think about it, I feel certain that I've never seen him before in my life. One day, he was in my dream, and the next day— *He was in my way.* I'm honestly worried that I might be hallucinating him. And that's not all; I've been hearing voices and smelling things that aren't around me. He says he's real, but he can't be. Has anything like this ever— I mean, could this be the fever or the elixir? I— help me!" Sawyer's panic had morphed her voice into a high-pitched shrill thing she barely recognized— every sentence higher, faster, and louder than the last.

"Okay, untwist your knickers — I'm coming. Don't leave your room and call me if you see him again. I should be there in twenty minutes."

Kaelan looked like a man unraveled by hardship, as they pulled out of the parking lot and headed towards whatever he was so impatient to show her. He stopped at a red light and took a couple of deep breaths before he spoke again.

"Okay, first, know that I am of sound mind." The light turned green and he took a right.

"You're not crazy, got it." They took a quick left.

"And you trust me, correct?"

"Of course I trust you. Wait, should I *not* trust you? What's going on?" Her question went unanswered until they got to their location, which turned out not to be that far away.

Kaelan turned onto a street with the entrance sign, "Greek Row". It was filled with sororities on one side and fraternities on the other. They stopped in front of a random sorority house.

"You know, walking would have been shorter, right? I could see this place from the quad. Why did we drive over here?"

His next words came rushing out; a jumbled mess in his hurry to say everything he needed to say as quickly as possible.

"SodontfreakoutbutIwascomingback-
fromthelibrabyandfoundyourdoogelgan-
agerand—"

"You found my what?"

"Your doppelganger!"

"What do you mean *my* doppelganger?"
Sam raised an eyebrow at him.

"She looks exactly like you." He eyed the
houses lining the street. "She's somewhere here and
we need to find her so I can show you!"

"Okay. Right." Sam paused, pursing her lips
together. "And how do you know she's on this
street, exactly?"

"Well, I bumped into her and then watched
her go this way when I went to get you from
the car. And before you say it, yes, I know," He
admitted sheepishly.

"Well, I'm going to say it anyway. Stalking
is *bad* but we'll have a nice, long discussion about
boundaries later." Sam smirked as she opened the
car door, following Kaelan onto the street.

He pulled the fob out of his pocket and
locked the doors, before taking her hand in his.

"Ready?"

"Not remotely."

The street was energetic. From what she could hear, it appeared like a number of parties were going on at once. A variety of different types of music flooded the air, assaulting her ears from multiple directions as they blurred together into an indecipherable concoction.

Some houses had strobe lights bursting through every window, while a number of them were bathed in coloured flood lighting on both their interiors and exteriors. Most of them had lines out the door. Flyers littered the sidewalks and Sam read a few as they walked around: a bright purple piece of paper where the words, 'End of Sem: Party Harty', were displayed in black font, and a neon pink one with the headline: "Sawyer Didn't Die So Stop By!" splashed across the center in white. Sam thought about the unfortunate people who'd have to clean the street in the morning, as she stepped over a light blue, Gamma-something poster.

Sam suppressed her blossoming apprehension as they approached the first house; squeezing Kaelan's hand a little tighter for comfort.

"Let's go find an impostor!"

Sam and Kaelan didn't stop at house number one since the party was still being set up. But they hadn't gone much farther than that when people started talking to her.

"Cute outfit, Sawyer. Very different. Is the party themed?"

"Ouuu, I hope it is!"

"And who is *he*?"

Women fired questions and statements at her from all directions as she continued walking. She started slowly piecing information together as they moved.

"Everyone seems to think I'm this 'Sawyer' person?" she whispered to Kaelan.

She could admit that this was strange — she would have to give Kaelan that. But before she could overthink it, Kaelan was pulling her up some steps that led to giant French doors. She looked up at the giant Greek lettering that adorned the house.

"You saw the flyer and figured it out too then." She chuckled at his anticipation as he dragged her up the steps, her shorter legs unable to keep up with his long strides.

They burst through the doors, shifting some of the balloons that were cluttered all over the floor. Once inside, he let go of her hand and disappeared without a word; she was standing alone in the grand foyer.

"Where are you going?" She called after him, but he was so fixated on his new destination he didn't respond.

This is absolutely ridiculous.

The house was precisely what she expected from a sorority, but a lot less "Barbie" than she thought it would be. There was a lot of bone white décor and pastel palettes throughout the interior — mostly soft sage and champagne, while the statement pieces were all different shades of warm browns. A giant staircase took up one side of the entryway, and an impressive, *very modern,* tiered chandelier was hanging extravagantly from the ceiling. Two plush white couches were placed right below the chandelier— in between them, a tall, pampas grass display stood in a ceramic floor-vase. Apart from what looked like a small, in-house café, the rest of the house was tucked away behind crystal sliding doors and solid drapes.

"I asked some girl for your room. Well, I asked for *Sawyer's* room. She told me it's the sixth one on the right."

"Very trusting with personal information in this part of the world, I see — it's not like you're a stalker or anything." She hit his hand playfully as they started up the stairs.

Part of her started wondering if this was something Kaelan had planned. It was possible that he was trying to distract her from some elaborate proposal he had put together. She looked back at him; exhilaration brightening his face. He was definitely great at pretending to be caught up in this whole thing.

If this isn't a prank, then this whole situation might be the most uncanny thing that's ever happened to me.

They made it to the top of the staircase and walked down the hall. Sam counted the doors as they passed them.

One.

Two.

Three.

Four.

Five.

Six.

Ready or not, here I come.

8

No Fricking Idea

SAWYER

SAWYER WAS MESSAGING MADDIE, and looking through the window from her favourite viewing spot on the bed, when she heard a knock at her door.

There was another knock at the door, this time more insistent.

She bounced off her bed and rushed over to open the door, wondering how Imogen had gotten there so quickly. Sawyer had just turned the knob when the man from earlier busted through the door of her bedroom. She stepped back, wanting to put some distance between her and her would-be assailant.

She screamed, scrambling over to her bed to grab her phone. "I'm gonna call the police!" She tripped over her backpack, heart racing— she needed to get to her phone on the nightstand where she'd put it down.

The man seemed to be in no hurry to attack her, giving Sawyer the opportunity to get to the phone in record time. She picked it up, desperate to call for help. But before she could tap the screen and swipe up for the emergency button, it slipped through her shaking fingers, landing face down on the carpeted floor.

She felt her vision blurring, dancing black spots were impairing her sight. She could feel herself starting to hyperventilate as white hot tears pricked her eyes.

Who let him up here?! How the fuck did he find me?

"DID YOU FOLLOW ME?!"

Of course he followed me!

"Help! Somebody hel—" Sawyer was shrieking.

"NO! Don't call the cops— SAM! *Please* stop screaming— SAM!!" He was as panicked as she was, and he kept glancing between Sawyer and the door. "This is just a misunderstanding, I swear! SAM!!!"

Sawyer extended her leg and used her foot to sweep the fallen phone closer to her. She bent over and picked it up, keeping her hazy vision trained on the man in front of her.

"Calm down, I'm coming! I was just looking at a painting on the wall but—"

"SAMANTHA!"

"Imma need you to stop yelling at me!"

He actually *has a girlfriend?*

Sawyer was starting to relax, her heart rate slowing down from its previous frenzy.

"You weren't lying about having a girlfriend? I thought—" Sawyer's words cut off abruptly as Sam stepped through the bedroom door.

An unnatural stillness filled the room as the two women stared at each other.

No fucking way.

Sawyer and Sam stepped forward until they were a foot apart, watching each other in a mesmerized stupor.

"What the actual *fuck*?" Sam was the first to break the silence.

"Absolutely not. Nope. NOPE! I'm not dealing with *this shit* right now." Sawyer paced back and forth, pivoting between Sam and the foot of her bed.

"Can you stop pacing? It's stressing me out. And I'm already stressed the fuck out."

Sawyer ignored her, mumbling to herself as she continued her pacing.

Sam turned to Kaelan, who kept glancing back and forth between the women.

"I thought I'd realized just how alike you two were before, but now? I don't actually believe it," he was saying, semi-stunned.

"This isn't real. This isn't real. This cannot be happening," Sawyer whispered over and over as she slowly wrapped her arms around herself, still pacing.

"It feels like I'm about to freak out — she's *obviously* already freaking out — and I don't want to deal with it." Sam moved closer to Kaelan, whispering, "I've seen her. She does look a lot like me. Now can we leave?"

"This can't be happeni—"

"Just fucking *stay still* for five minutes and breathe!" Sam snapped, reaching out to grab Sawyer so she could stop her from moving. "Or do I need to bitch slap you to bring you back to reality?"

Sam only held on to her in an attempt to quell the meltdown the other woman was having, but when their skin touched, an icy blue dome appeared around overhead, encasing them.

"Sawyer?! Sawyer!"

Imogen was screaming as she rushed through the door towards the dome. She extended her hand towards the radiant blue orb in an attempt to test for a way in. When her hand touched the surface, she was thrown into a wall across the room, an electrical surge shooting out from the dome. It glowed intensely, energetically pulsing through the room and erupting goosebumps over everyone's skin.

Kaelan ran over to the newcomer, closing and locking the door to prevent anyone else from stumbling in. He offered her a hand to help her up.

"Are you okay?"

"I think so. Knocked the wind straight out of me." Imogen's eyes never left the orb, even as she took his hand and was hoisted off the ground, her breathing unsteady.

"I'm Kaelan, and that," he pointed to the luminous bubble, "is my girlfriend, Samantha."

Imogen cautiously walked towards the dome once more — she made sure not to touch it this time.

"Name's Imogen, and that's my mate, Sawyer." She moved around the orb to inspect both women, who were standing unnaturally still on the inside.

"Why does your girlfriend look exactly like her?" She asked the question without turning to face him.

"We actually have no fricking idea."

The silence lingered past the point of comfortability. Neither woman had spoken a word after their unexplainable relocation from Sawyer's bedroom to an unknown destination.

The brisk wind was invigorating — it danced around them, tugging at their clothes and throwing their curly hair around. Multiple choruses from a variety of birds echoed from the too-tall treetops. The sun stretched across swaying branches, splashing the forest floor with long, dancing shadows.

Sawyer craned her neck upwards to look at the tiny pieces of blue sky she could see peeping through the canopy of trees. "So, this is what having a psychotic break is like. Not bad, I guess."

Samantha mimicked Sawyer's actions and gazed up into the trees.

"Either this is some serious denial, or she's not as smart as she looks. And what the hell is she looking at?"

"Did you just call me stupid?"

"I didn't call you anything."

The realization that neither of them had spoken out loud before this moment dawned on them simultaneously.

"This isn't even a little bit cliché at all." Sam rolled her eyes. "I'm pretty sure I've read or watched this exact plot device, only *everywhere*."

Her sarcasm and mannerisms reminded Sawyer a little of Iyana. She started to respond to her but was distracted by chants coming from their left.

"Quick, get behind that." Sam pointed towards a fallen tree trunk and they both hurried and nestled behind it.

"Death to the devil's enchantress!"

"Kill the demon temptress!"

"Burn, witch, burn!"

They watched as a woman ran through the trees, passing directly in front of them as she stumbled, regained her footing, and tried not to trip again — a task made more difficult by her swift glances at the mob pursuing her.

The woman spotted a hill and barreled towards it. Not looking back this time, she started climbing, clutching her visibly pregnant stomach as tears streamed down her face. She scraped her knee against the rough terrain, scrambling up the incline. The woman slowed for a few seconds, attempting to catch her breath. Then she started moving again, using a lateral branch to pull herself to the top, she disappeared over the crest.

Sam and Sawyer followed her carefully, not sure if they could be seen by anyone. The hill was steeper than it looked, but they made it to the top swiftly and found a place to watch the events unfold. The crest of the hill plateaued into the entry point of a village. There was a large, unpaved road dividing the town into two halves. Sawyer and Sam had lost sight of the woman, having waited too long to follow her. They ran towards the right side of the road, shielding themselves by hugging the side of an apothecary. The buildings in view all looked like businesses, not housing, and none of them seemed to be open yet.

"We could sneak along the fronts of the buildings and try to find her." Sam nodded her head in the direction she thought they should go. "What do you think?"

"I think I want to go home!" Sawyer whispered loudly.

"Great, she's also a scaredy-cat."

"Hey, I heard that!"

But Sam didn't respond, she kept looking for the woman.

Sawyer watched the mob starting to clear the hill as Sam spotted the woman darting behind a building on the other side of the road.

"Let's go." Sam stepped out before Sawyer could stop her and ended up just a few feet away from the leader of the crowd.

Sam breathed out slowly, sliding her hand into her back pocket to retrieve her switchblade.

There was nothing there. She reached inward, summoning her power, and nothing responded.

Fuck.

She didn't know if she should retreat. She had no powers and no weapons, so the fight would be hand to hand. The man had at least thirty pounds on her. But the closer he got, the more she noticed that he didn't appear to be looking *at* her. When they were face to face, he hesitated for a brief second before walking straight through her.

"They can't see us!" Sam called to Sawyer, resuming her pursuit of the woman, not waiting to see if Sawyer would follow along.

The hateful screams of the group felt more imposing against the silence of the still sleeping town. The disgust in their voices bellowed in the distance, the chorus continued to taunt their victim, as they moved down the center of the giant road. They knocked on doors as they went, calling for the town's people to surrender the woman and repent.

Sawyer was across the road now. She followed Sam, who was following the alleged pregnant witch. It was easier to move around now that she knew no one could see them. She caught up to them relatively quickly.

"Where the hell are we?"

"More like *when* are we," Sam responded, not bothering to look at Sawyer as she ran up alongside her.

The environment was a dead giveaway that they weren't where they were supposed to be. Even the clothes of the mob members looked like they had been plucked from the pages of a history book. The realization pushed forcefully against Sawyer's wall of denial as she surveyed their surroundings in detail. When she turned to respond, she realized she was standing alone as her look-alike had started off after the woman again. She seemed to be headed in the opposite direction to the growing mob. The horde was moving further away, taking their yelling with them, but they would soon run out of places to search and double-back in their efforts.

Sam followed closely behind as the woman hustled up to a house with a blue front door and knocked three times, pausing before she knocked twice more. The next pause was longer than the first, then she knocked two more times. The door swung open to let her in and Samantha slipped in behind her. Sawyer had just gotten to the threshold of the door when Sam's hand reached for her and dragged her inside before the door was closed. The house was small and further away from the rest of the community. It should be a little while before the mob reached their location, even if they had already started to turn back.

"What are you doing?" Sawyer asked, normally now, instead of whispering.

"Shhh!"

She was offended by the shushing. "If they can't see us then I doubt they can hear us."

"I'm not afraid we'll get caught. I'm trying to listen." Sam shrugged, a little miffed.

Sam briefly side eyed the young woman who looked just like her, then resumed watching the pregnant woman. This was the first time Sam had noticed how beautiful the woman was, in spite of how tired she was — the dark circles under her eyes indicated her severe lack of sleep. There was dirt smeared on her face, and her clothes hadn't been washed in a while. Sam could see scrapes and gashes along the woman's hands, legs, and knees — some were starting to heal and others had now been opened up. The pregnant woman hung on to the edge of the windowsill, her knuckles white under the pressure she was using to hold her exhausted body up.

"You have to help me! My baby, she's coming!"

At first, Sam thought the woman was talking to them, but then an elderly woman emerged from the shadows. Her eyes were kind, and her hair was done in two French braids on each side of her head that stopped in the middle of her back. She had a barely noticeable limp and squinted slightly as she walked, even though it was still bright outside.

"Come on then, child, and hurry."

Struggling to move, as quickly as she could with her stomach cradled in her arms, she hobbled after the elderly woman, who grabbed onto her arm and led her into a hidden underground room. Sawyer and Sam followed behind in silence. The soil in the floor-less basement room was damp, sending smells of wet earth through the entire space. When they entered, there were three more women waiting to assist. Two of them immediately helped the pregnant woman onto a table while the third started gathering supplies.

As they prepared for the birth of her baby, pounding echoed from the door above. The noise made Sawyer's heart stop and tears began to form in her eyes with the realization that this woman and her child might not survive.

"Try to keep quiet — if they find out you're here, they will kill us all."

The old woman slipped out of the room and one of the others followed behind her to bolt the door close. Footsteps and muffled voices overhead made the woman in labour freeze. She glanced up nervously, trying even harder than she already was to mask her pain, and covered her mouth with a cloth to suppress her screams. Sweat glistened on her forehead as she groaned through another contraction.

They could partially hear the old woman's yelling, but the sounds of slamming drawers and tumbling furniture were drowning out her voice. Stampede-like stomps and a magnitude of crashes kept thundering into the underground space. Sawyer and Sam looked at each other, with the understanding that some of the mob were most likely tearing the woman's small house apart in their search. Then, there was a scuffle above that made everyone in the delivery room hold their breath. A loud and unexpected pop rang out, then they could hear the shuffle of feet moving towards the front door.

"Don't worry, we're safe down here. The entrance to the room is well hidden," one of the women tearfully whispered reassurances to the pregnant woman.

A few moments later, the door slammed closed; the invaders had left empty-handed. The room exhaled a collective sigh of saddened relief.

Sam had never taken her eyes off the woman on the table.

The elderly woman never returned.

"The baby's coming," she whispered so softly, Sawyer almost didn't hear.

Sam and Sawyer watched with bated breath as the woman continued her arduous labour and delivery. It didn't take long, and after twenty minutes or so, Sawyer stood amazed at how tiny, peaceful, and beautiful the newborn baby girl was. So blissfully unaffected by the horror that preceded her birth.

"She's absolutely perfect."

"I think she looks like a kitten and she's all wrinkly," Sam muttered to Sawyer.

"Well, you'd be wrong. She's darling," Sawyer replied, focusing on the baby instead. And as she gazed at the little bundle, she couldn't help but wonder what was going to happen to the baby and her mother.

Listening to the crying newborn, Sam thought about how incredible it was that these women had helped this expectant mother and risked their lives to make sure she could deliver her baby. She watched the new mother physically relax and finally smile as she looked at her daughter.

"Welcome to the cruel world, my precious Dayana."

Sawyer and Sam smiled at each other before they were dragged from one timeline and dropped into another one.

They now stood in a spectacular house with extremely high ceilings and large floor-length windows. Their blurred reflections looked back at them from the surface of the polished, ebony, ash wood floors. The abstract black and white photographs jumped off the Tinsmith Gray walls, each clear, acrylic frame separated by brushed brass wall sconces.

The home was a sophisticated one — through pure white drapes they could see that they were perched on a hill surrounded by Red Spruce trees. Both women walked towards the window so they could clearly see the view below. A monstrous river moved along the left of the forest, its mouth opening up into a crystal-clear lake.

"Where are we?" They asked simultaneously.

Their question was answered when a woman came torpedoing around a corner, grabbing their attention — they swiveled their heads around to watch her run.

"They're coming!" An older woman, who was hurrying after the human missile that had just passed by, exclaimed to a third lady walking through the front door.

The two women quickly made their way down the hallway, following the same path as the running lady. Their steps turning into a partial jog as they entered an empty room and started rapidly setting up a bed and prepping medical equipment.

"Nothing like a little bit of déjà vu," Sam said quietly as the two of them walked into the room. She paused, turning to the girl next to her. "Wait, what's your name?"

Sawyer hesitated, then responded, "Sawyer. What's yours?"

"The hesitation was a little weird, Sawyer," Sam chuckled as they posted up on a wall near the entrance of the room.

"Well, I thought about it and figured you might have known,"

"How?" Sam side-eyed her a little.

"You can read my mind, can't you?"

"I can hear your thoughts, which I don't think is the same as reading your mind. I mean, I can't seem to hear you *all* the time. Can you hear what I'm thinking right now?"

"No." She was a little embarrassed, though that didn't seem to be the other woman's intention.

"I'm Samantha, by the way." She smiled at Sawyer and felt some of the tension melt away. The two turned their attention back to the bed, watching the three women finish setting up the delivery room, when a couple, including a very pregnant woman, hustled through the door.

"Mom, hi! I'm terrified." The woman chuckled anxiously as she climbed on the bed, still holding the man's hand.

Sam spotted their wedding bands and nudged Sawyer softly with her elbow.

"That's the husband." She'd resumed whispering — in the midst of the activity around them, speaking loudly felt like it was against the rules.

Sawyer eyed the couple, her gaze moving from the wife to the husband, and then back again.

"I'm here, baby, and soon our girls will be too," the woman's husband responded as he cupped her face, kissing her sweaty forehead and smiling at her with a loving gaze. The woman smiled back and took a deep breath as she bent her knees, preparing to push.

"All ready to go, miss Renee Dayana," her mom and obstetrician chuckled lightly, "because here come Samantha, Sawyer and Sadie."

9
Children of the Universe

SAWYER AND SAMANTHA MARVELED at each other with the understanding that they were about to watch their birth.

"I didn't know I was adopted." Sawyer's voice was so small Sam had almost missed it. She reached out and laced their fingers together.

"Does it make this more difficult to see?"

"I, I don't know." Her response was barely audible as she gripped Sam's hand more forcefully.

Neither of them spoke again as they witnessed the moment unfolding. If there had been any doubt left for either of them, it was destroyed now. They were sisters and there was another one of them out there.

Watching their mother and father was overwhelming for them both: Sawyer, who never knew that her parents weren't actually her biological parents, and Sam, who never thought she would ever know where she'd come from.

The first cry resonated through the room that had so far only been filled with their mother's groans and their father's encouragement. It shattered the tension that had been holding the young women together.

"Hello, Samantha." Their father's smooth, deep voice mixed with their mother's short laughs, making Sawyer teary-eyed. She squeezed Sam's hand even tighter and felt comforted when her sister squeezed back.

"*I have a sister.*"

"*You have two sisters.*" Sam smiled at Sawyer who was no longer just teary-eyed; she'd started crying.

"Let's check to make sure baby number two is in the right position before she starts to come." Their grandmother felt their mother's abdomen before reaching for the bedside ultrasound.

"How's it looking mom?"

"She looks great. It should be any minute now." Their grandmother got back in position.

Three minutes later, another cry joined baby Samantha's, the two voices ringing in unison throughout the delivery room.

"Baby Sawyer's here!" Their father was laughing almost hysterically, joy plastered across his face.

"How do they look? Are they doing okay?" Their mother asked from the delivery bed as the midwives checked the babies' vitals.

"They're the most beautiful girls I have ever seen, Renee. And they're doing great. But we've still got one more to go."

Their grandmother repeated the same steps as before. Sam and Sawyer watched on as their sister was about to be born. A couple minutes passed. Then another five went by. They watched their mother laboriously deliver the last of the trio, as everyone waited anxiously to meet her, but their anticipation of her cries was met with silence.

An eternity of stillness smothered the space, before their mother's pained wail filled every crevice of the delivery room, echoing through the vast hallways. The baby laid motionless, cradled in their grandmother's arms. The two midwives present rushed over and assisted in trying to revive

Sadie; their efforts soon became a lesson in futility. Their father looked back and forth between his broken wife and his beautiful daughters, quiet tears rolling down his cheeks. Their grandmother, still dressed in her medical scrubs, rocked her crying daughter in her arms. Baby Sam and baby Sawyer cried as loud as their little lungs allowed them, seemingly mourning the part of them they'd lost, as present-day Sam and Sawyer stood plastered to the delivery room wall where they were crying too.

In the midst of their grief, a faint light began radiating from Sadie's little body. Soon, the incandescent glow had grown and surrounded her, warming the air around her before it began to drain away. The light danced and sparkled off her skin, then divided into two glowing orbs which hovered in the air.

"What's happening?" Their mother's voice cracked with emotion as she strained to get a clearer view.

But no one answered, transfixed by the strange energy making its way from Sadie to the other two babies.

"Stop it! Don't let it hurt them!" Their mother was struggling in her attempt to get out of bed so she could intervene.

"Just wait, dear, I don't think their sister plans to hurt them."

Their grandmother had never seen it happen before, but she'd read an ancient text once that spoke about power lending and transference between siblings. It was such a rare occurrence that there wasn't substantial documentation to explain how or why it happened.

Sadie's power danced around Sam and Sawyer's tiny frames, turning their cries into coos. Sam began to glow like Sadie had before — incandescent colors twinkling along her skin. Then it began happening to Sawyer.

"She's giving them her powers," their mother whispered before she passed out.

"Sam?!"

"Sawyer!"

It took a few moments for them to snap out of their trance and gain lucidity. They looked at each other, then around at their surroundings, noting that they were finally back in Sawyer's bedroom.

Kaelan and Imogen stood screaming their names, panic contorting their features. Sawyer reached out to touch the surface of the swirling, blue dome that held her and her sister captive.

"*You're braver than I thought.*" A small smile played on Sam's lips as Sawyer placed her palm along the inside of the bubble.

A mellow breeze rippled through the inside of the room and the glowing orb began to pulse, growing brighter for a second before it began to dematerialize slowly. Sam joined Sawyer and placed her hand on the surface of the orb, feeling its fading warmth. A moment after, it completely vanished.

"Are you okay?!" Kaelan and Imogen asked in unison.

"I—, she—, we—," Sawyer looked around frantically before passing out.

Imogen sprinted over to her and barely prevented Sawyer from splitting her head open on the edge of her bed frame. She grabbed the sweater from the back of a computer chair and bundled it under Sawyer's head before looking behind her to see what was happening to the other Sawyer.

"Sam, talk to me."

Sam glanced at Sawyer's unconscious body then turned around to face Kaelan.

"We—, I saw—,"

Sam fainted on the opposite side of her sister but Kaelan was close enough to catch her before she went down. He scooped her legs up into his arms and cradled her against his body.

Kaelan looked at his girlfriend, then to her lookalike, before turning to Imogen who was now squatting on the floor, next to the unconscious woman.

"So, what now?" he asked, continuously looking between the two.

"Now, we take them back to my house, love," Imogen replied before lifting Sawyer off the ground, surprising Kaelan with the strength she had in such a dainty frame.

"Let's get on then."

When Sam woke up, she was hit by a wave of uncontrollable emotion. She sat up frantically and tried to get her bearings as she looked around the room she didn't recognize. The throbbing behind her left eye told her a massive headache was on its way. She shifted under the sheets as the events of the past couple hours flooded her brain. When she finally snapped out of her daze, Sam scanned the room and spotted a sleeping, or possibly unconscious body, lying in the bed on the opposite side of the room. She remembered seeing Sawyer faint and assumed that it must be her sister in the bed across from her.

There were only two beds in the room and they were exactly the same— king-sized with sleek, gold posts at each corner of the bed frame. The posts themselves were embellished with tribal engravings etched along their surface. Following the pattern with her eyes, she realized that the markings had started from the base of the post and traveled up the entire length until they merged together, creating a golden ratio spiral in the middle of the canopy frame. It glittered overhead, the flecks of gold so mesmerizing they appeared to move. The bedding was plain ivory, which in its simplicity, added another layer of subtle sophistication to the room. It took her a moment to look past the beauty of the bed through sheer curtains hanging from the canopy's sides.

Remarkable.

Beyond the bed was a vast and exquisite room. There was a large cappuccino-colored rug with a giant golden ratio spiral, made from the image of twinkling stars, adorning the center of the room. It complemented the dark brown varnished floors and Mystic Gold walls. Intricate paintings were hung throughout the room, but what stood out the most, was a group of black words that had been beautifully scripted onto a colossal, cream, accent wall, back lit by a soft, golden light.

Sam hadn't even realized she had gotten up and walked across the entire length of the room until she was standing directly in front of the wall, gazing up at the words:

We are the beginning and the end. Ethe- real and Primordial. We are light in the darkness. Created to restore what is lost

She had just finished reading when movement behind her shifted her focus. Turning around, she looked straight into the teary eyes of her sister — they looked so much like her own.

"Where are we?" Sawyer asked, pinching the bridge of her nose between her eyes in what was possibly an attempt to stop more tears from falling.

"I have no idea." Sam walked back to bed and fell face forward into a pile of pillows, groaning loudly.

"*Neither of us knows where we are. This is fucking fantastic.*"

"Tell me about it," Sawyer replied, throwing herself across the bed next to Sam.

Kaelan

The five of them kept glancing around at each other. It was a long time before anyone said anything. Kaelan was sitting at a distance from everyone else when the woman with the indescribable hair broke the silence.

"So," she stretched the word so that it lingered in the air. "There's two of them?" she asked in a thick Irish accent.

One of the women kept glancing over at the teenager, and the girl kept avoiding her by looking at the floor.

"I'll deal with you later." Her voice was laced with disappointment. "Do you know how dangerous what you did was?"

The girl was fiddling with the strap of her shirt; her head, still down.

Kaelan watched as the woman exasperatedly ran her hands through her hair. She exhaled deeply just as the girl looked up at her.

"Never mind. Like I said, we'll discuss this later." She seemed to be trying to convince herself that she could hold off the reprimand.

No one had answered the question about Sam and her lookalike. And after the latest

one-sided conversation, silence descended heav-
ily, suffocating the room. Everyone was lost in
thought, so Kaelan directed his question towards no
one in particular and hoped that the girl, or any of
the women currently present, would answer it.

"Does anyone plan to talk about what's
happening, or are we just going to sit here memo-
rizing each other's faces a bit longer?" He was tired
of not knowing who these women were or where
they took Sam.

If the petite one from before hadn't told
him with such confidence that they could help
Samantha, he would have never brought her here.
He didn't know if he had made the right decision
in trusting them because he hadn't seen Sam since
they'd "taken her to rest".

Now, he and the woman he loved were in
a place they didn't know, with a bunch of people
he didn't know. He sighed, remembering the fear
he felt seeing Sam unconscious in his arms. In that
moment, keeping her with the only person who
had experienced the same thing as her, seemed like
the best thing to do. Especially because he himself
had absolutely no idea what that experience was.

"Well—" A woman with curly brown hair
and amber eyes started to talk before she was cut
off.

"Iyana, I'll take it from here since your approach tends to be proper abrasive sometimes, love."

Kaelan looked at the woman, who had stood up and was now walking towards him. She was the smallest of the bunch and looked a lot like the girl whose name he couldn't remember. At first, he thought they were identical twins too, but once he'd seen them up close, their differences jumped out at him. Smiling, she motioned for him to join her. He obliged and followed her, where they ended up sitting next to each other on a couch that was further away from the others. It was directly in front of one of the most impressive glass windows he had ever seen in his life. The view overlooked a sea of different fir and pine trees, framed by mountain top silhouettes. If it weren't for the pit of worry bubbling in his stomach, he would have been able to appreciate it more.

"My name is Anabelle. I don't think we've been formally introduced. There is a lot you need to know, and I have to ask you to keep an open mind and listen carefully."

Kaelan nodded and so she continued.

IO

Sounds Intense

IMOGEN

"I WONDER WHAT SHE'S saying to him." Amira switched seats from where she previously was, to sit on the end of the loveseat, squeezing herself between Iyana and Imogen.

"Girl, I don't care. Wuh I waan know is wuh *dis* one find out 'bout Mary-Kate and Ashley."

Imogen rolled her eyes at the comment, a tiny smirk on her face. "I don't know anything, really. Once I got there, everything was already happening." She toyed with the electric blue end of one of her locs.

"There's gotta be a story. Did you talk to the other one? What's her name? Is she anything like Sawyer?"

Amira's rapid-fire questions took them by surprise — Imogen and Iyana started uncontrollably laughing at her enthusiasm.

Imogen summarized the entire debacle from the very beginning. She made sure to pause for questions and interruptions, of which there were plenty.

"I don't think the other girl, I think her name is Sam, could hear either." She paused, using her head to point in the direction of Anabelle and Kaelan who were still talking on the bench. "He kept yelling for her but she didn't bat an eyelash in his direction."

"Well, shit."

"We were both gobsmacked, to be honest — neither of us knew what to do. We had to stand around and wait for them to snap out of it. It was about twenty minutes before either one stirred."

Amira and Iyana were hanging on to every word, afraid that even breathing too loud might disrupt her story.

"After the dome disappeared, the two of them just stood there like nothing had happened, until their eyes rolled back and they passed out. We didn't get to talk to either of them, so I figured it would be better to get them here." She waited for their reactions, as they stared at her astonished. "The end. I mean, well, you know the rest."

"Sounds intense."

"I still don't believe dem got two for real though."

Imogen laughed at how after the entire re-cap, Iyana's attention was on Sawyer having a twin sister.

But Iyana was probably thinking the same thing she was— Sam being Sawyer's twin meant that she probably had powers too. And if they were lucky, that would be a valuable addition to their team.

An extra Ethereal would reinforce the veil a lot more than only one. Even if this was currently speculation, both her and Anabelle had abilities. So, in theory, a set of twins would have to have magic too.

"Wait, anybody check to see wuh magic she got? Or if she got any at all?"

They all fell completely silent for a moment as all three eyed each other, then smiled. Imogen and Amira shot up from their seats and sprinted down the hall towards the room where Sam and Sawyer were asleep.

Iyana followed behind, chuckling as she walked, before yelling after them.

"Wunna so ridiculous!"

Imogen was still cracking up when she and Amira made it to the bedroom door.

Sawyer watched her sister roll over onto her back, running her hand over her face. She started making mental notes of Sam's mannerisms, watching for any similarities between them. Looking at Sam was a lot like looking in a mirror — that is, if she'd had a makeover and suddenly started dressing like Rihanna.

"So, we're sisters." Sawyer repositioned herself while absentmindedly running her fingers up and down the markings on the bedpost closest to her.

She watched as Sam crossed her legs and leaned against the tall footboard of the bed frame so she could sit facing her.

"More than sisters, we're twins."

"Well, triplets, assuming what we saw really happened." Sawyer finally stopped playing with the bedpost and looked into the eyes that contained the same sadness she knew were reflected in her own.

"Yeah, triplets."

The pain in her sister's voice was too clear to miss and Sawyer's heart ached with her over the sister they would never know. She looked over at the sister she'd found, in bittersweet reverie.

Sad smiles passed between them before Sam started speaking again.

"We've met, but I guess it wasn't official. Samantha, but everyone calls me Sam." Sam extended her hand towards Sawyer.

"Still just Sawyer over here. Not sure if there's a cute, abbreviated version of that." She reached out and shook her sister's hand.

"Well, Sawyer, whatever this is, we can figure it out together." Sam laughed lightly to mitigate the remaining sadness in the air.

Sawyer was about to ask Sam a question when the door to the room flew open. A woman and girl skidded in, almost dogpiling on top of each other when they slid to a stop.

"Amira? Imogen?"

"You know these people?"

"Barely," she whispered back.

"Oh, they're awake." It was hard to miss the disappointment in the statement.

"Doesn't mean we can't check still," Iyana said as she walked into the room.

Sam smirked, and Sawyer could already tell Sam liked Iyana, who didn't look friendly at all with her slight scowl.

"What are you guys doing here? And where is 'here' anyways? Are we back at your house?"

"She's ask so much questions. If de other one so too, I gine wait outside."

Sawyer curled up her lip at Iyana and rolled her eyes. Ignoring her was probably better than antagonizing her, so instead, she focused on getting answers from Imogen and Amira.

"Well, after you both fainted, I thought it would be a good idea to bring you back and let Anabelle help with your little situation," Imogen answered while walking a little further into the room, eyes trained on Samantha.

"Well, her 'little situation' is sitting right here, and — for your information — it can *hear* you."

Kaelan

Kaelan sighed when Anabelle had finished explaining everything to him. She wasn't kidding when she had told him it would be a lot to take in. Thankfully, he had known about Sam's gifts, so at least he didn't have a meltdown learning about them. The veils to different worlds and the demons ready to infest earth were an entirely different story.

At the end of her debrief, Anabelle had asked him to let her be the one to explain it all to Sam and Sawyer. He wasn't sure he could explain it so he didn't mind letting her take the lead. Then she told him he could see Sam. Anabelle led him down a long hallway into an ornately decorated room where he saw his girlfriend, her lookalike, and the three others from before standing in a circle of sorts.

"I'm not letting you push a thermometer in my mouth. I don't—," Sam stopped talking when she saw Kaelan enter the room. She ran to him and hopped into his arms, wrapping her legs around him and pulling him in for a kiss.

He grabbed on to her thighs, squeezing them gently as her body collided with his, kissing her back desperately.

"I didn't know you were here." She shimmied up his body a little bit, running her hands up his neck and into his hair before she kissed him again.

"Nothing is more important," they kissed again, "than making sure," another kiss broke his sentence apart, "you're safe."

"Ah, would ya stop! We're still here in case you lot forgot." The woman with the chocolate brown eyes and three-tone hair snapped him back to reality.

He gave Sam one more quick peck before he released her thighs, so she could hop off him. With her feet securely on the floor, she smiled and snuggled into his side. He cleared his throat in apology while Sam stood, unashamed, of their very public affection. Brown-eyes smiled at Sam's confidence.

Samantha stepped forward and waved at the group.

"Hey, I'm Sam," she announced, looking from woman to woman.

"Anabelle, nice to meet—" Anabelle's introduction was cut short when the woman with the Caribbean accent butt in.

"Amira, Imogen and Iyana." She pointed to each person as she introduced them. "Now that

we've got *that* out of the way," Iyana excitedly
shoved the thermometer at Sam and all but jammed
it down her throat, "open up."

She wiggled her eyebrows.

They had her try three different thermometers before they relented, unsatisfied with her normal temperature readings. Sam participated, although she was unsure of what they were trying to do.

"Can someone explain to me what's going on?"

"Oh. They're trying to see if you're hot like I was." It was Sawyer who answered.

"Hot like you?"

"Yeah, a fever almost killed me."

"It didn't almost *kill* you," Amira responded dismissively from where she stood in the circle.

"Wunna wasting time," Iyana interjected. Turning to Sam, she added, "We wanna see if you could do something like dis."

Iyana held out her left hand, her palm facing the ceiling.

Instantaneously, a ball of light formed above her skin, twirling around in the air and illuminating the circle formed by their bodies. It looked like she was holding a miniature version of the sun in her hand. Iyana was delighted with her production— she made it brighter, the light bleeding past the circle into the rest of the room. Then, she dimmed it until the light barely reached past the edge of her feet.

Sawyer was awed by the display of magic, finding Iyana's display more impressive than watching Amira grow flowers. She watched as Iyana snuffed out the heat-less sun in her hand, by calling it back to her and closing her palm around it.

"Oh." Sam laughed, her cavalier response stunning the other girls in the room.

They had expected her to react more like Sawyer did at first. Everyone looked back and forth between Sam and Kaelan— they'd expected a bigger reaction.

"Well, I can't do something exactly like that." She paused so her declaration could linger in the air a while before she continued. "But I can do something like this."

She held out her hands, facing them upwards like Iyana did, and blew air across the top of her palms.

Baby flurries danced out and swirled around the space where they stood. One landed on Imogen's cheek and she giggled. Unlike Iyana's sun, the flurries came with a chilled breeze which pushed them around before they melted against different surfaces.

The room was silent, all except the sound Kaelan's laughter coming from behind Anabelle.

Imogen spoke first; the shock of the moment kept the others silent. "You know about magic?"

Sam smiled, leaving the room in suspense for a moment, before answering, "I've known almost my whole life. Why?"

Sam looked at Sawyer. *"You haven't always known?"*

"No, I just found out. I thought this was all fake at first."

"Fake? How?" Sam chuckled when she asked Sawyer out loud, forgetting that they were having a private conversation.

"Wait, can you read each other's minds?" Anabelle asked, stepping forward to stand closer to the twin.

"I don't think so, but we can communicate telepathically. I don't know what she's thinking all the time. No deep dark secrets, nothing like that."

Sam winked at Sawyer and continued speaking for both of them. Sawyer was glad since she didn't think she had anything to add. She hadn't considered that telepathic communication wasn't

the same as mind reading before her sister pointed it out.

"It started after we got trapped in the orb,
but it seems like it's still going on, out here in the
real world," Sam continued.

"Interesting. I wonder what else you can
do." Anabelle's eyes lit up with fascination.

Anabelle expressed wanting both Sam *and*
Sawyer to move into their house for a while. At
least she had been completely honest about being
interested in finding out what powers the pair
held, and about also needing their help strength-
ening the veil against the threats they faced.

"We're only here for Kaelan's job; we
can't just move here. We don't even know you."
They had all relocated to the living room for the
discussion.

"I know it's a crazy thing to ask, but we
need to have the joining ceremony before it's
too late. We can't do that until you completely
come into your power." Anabelle's gaze drifted to

Sawyer, though Sam's objections were the ones being discussed.

"We don't even know what you can do together, and we *need* to find out." Anabelle continued, not wanting to wait for more interruptions.

"This entire thing is unhinged. We don't know you. I'm not going to move in." Sawyer was trying to be diplomatic so she wouldn't start a fight, but she was not signing up to save the world — she was still in school, for heaven's sake.

"Oh it's 'we' now? You din' just find out you had a sister? " Iyana retorted.

"Doesn't matter when she found out, I'm still her sister," Sam snapped in Sawyer's defense.

"You was *just* calling Imogen fuh help, but *now*, de shoe on de other foot so you can't be bothered?"

"I thought I was dying from your magic elixir!"

"You *were* dying — from the fever! You should be thankful we bothered to save you at all!" Amira chimed in.

"You only *saved* me because you *need* me!"

"Wait, I thought a minute ago she *wasn't* dying," Sam asked, her tone accusatory.

The women were butting heads, none of them relenting. Sawyer and Iyana kept going at it and Sam was constantly interceding in Sawyer's defense.

Imogen, Kaelan, and Anabelle hadn't said much of anything after the argument had begun. But Kaelan had subconsciously moved closer to Sam and Sawyer; Imogen shifted to stand nearer to Amira and Iyana. Anabelle alone, stood near the front of the room between the two groups. She finally interjected when it was clear the others were nowhere close to resolving their disagreement.

"If everyone could take a minute and *relax*. This is pointless." She turned her attention to Sam and Sawyer. "We can't force you to stay, but there's something you need to see."

She motioned for them to follow her, leaving the others behind. The three of them — Sawyer, Sam and Kaelan — trailed after her until they walked into a war room. One of the walls had the same large windows as the living room, but all the others were covered in screens or whiteboards.

The walls were painted in light steel blue, and the floor was dark walnut hardwood. A giant, rectangular table with a glass top was positioned in the center of the room, every side of it lined with eggshell-coloured, velvet rolling chairs. There was a notepad in front of every chair, and in the center of the table was an acrylic, cylinder vase filled with white roses. Granite countertops containing a coffee machine and snacks lined one of the walls, and a chiller for bottled water was located in the corner of the room, closest to the door.

"You can sit anywhere," Anabelle instructed as she hit a button to lower the automatic window shades. She turned on the screens and waited for them to get comfortable before she began.

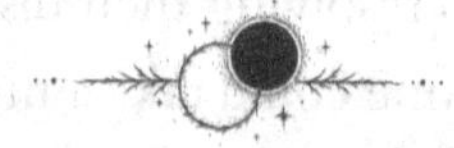

"According to the ancient text, over a millennia ago, the Universe gifted humans with unique abilities to aid her in the protection of the world." Anabelle changed the images on the screen in rapid succession, showing a variety of atrocities pulled from different time periods. "Long before anything you see here, humans showed her that they would do anything, and hurt anyone, to accumulate more power. And so, the universe took her magic back."

Kaelan had been briefed before but he was still as enthralled as the two sisters, who kept their eyes fixed on Anabelle.

"But the universe didn't leave humanity unprotected. Instead, she hand-selected a few of her daughters to serve as the earth's protectors. Passing down the magic and knowledge they," she hesitated, "*We,* would need to continue keeping everyone safe."

"Safe from what?" Goosebumps raised on Sawyer's arms — she wasn't sure she was ready for the answer.

"Demons." Anabelle's response was swift, accompanied by a slew of new images on the screens.

"These pictures were scanned in from the ancient books we own. But we don't know if the images are accurate." She looked at Sam who nodded for her to continue, ignoring the small squeak from Sawyer.

"There are a number of worlds that share our reality. And in all the worlds, humans are the weakest creatures to exist. When the Universe realized how much danger humanity was in, she constructed the veils to aid with our protection. And that's where we come in." Anabelle paused and looked around the room.

"Don't stop now, A. Bring it home." Kaelan smiled at Sam's bravery.

"Well," Anabelle chuckled, "Our job is to make sure the veils stay up — especially the veils between certain worlds, and most importantly, the veil between us and the demons. The Ethereals aren't always needed, we awaken when the veils begin to thin. Over the last five years, each of us has been gifted with magic. Or maybe, we always had it and just didn't know."

Sam and Sawyer exchanged looks.

Anabelle continued, "We have to renew the strength of the veil before it becomes thin enough for a demon army to completely break through and expand their realm onto our world. We've already seen reports of increased violence and unexplained attacks." Anabelle switched the images again and Sawyer got up to gag into the trash bin near the windows.

Sam glanced over at her sympathetically when she returned to her seat.

"When we noticed Sawyer, we started preparing for the joining ritual — as the fire Ethereal, the integration of your magic is required as the final piece of the group before we repair the veil. I don't know why we didn't see you too, Sam. Maybe because, technically, only one of you should exist. Unless, no nevermind. That can't be it," Anabelle was half talking to herself, half talking to them. "It shouldn't be too difficult to adapt the ceremony for two. I know it's a lot, but this is what we were put here to do, and if we don't, then the world as we know it won't exist for much longer."

II
Whatever You Decide

SAMANTHA

WITHOUT A WORD, SAWYER got up and stormed out of the room. Sam tried to push a thought towards her but was met with a wall. She tried to reach out to see if she could hear anything from Sawyer and got only silence. Her sister may be new to this telepathy business, but she had nailed the silent treatment.

Sam offered Anabelle a supportive look. "Anything else you wanna add before I go after her?"

"Just that we desperately need you. We can't do this alone. I know Sawyer is having a hard time, but will you at least *consider* joining us?"

Samantha looked to Kaelan, who had remained silent during the entire briefing.

"I'll stand by you, whatever you decide."

Sam nodded. "Then I'm in. If we're the only hope at preventing the destruction of our world. I'll help, and I'll see if I can convince Sawyer too." Sam pushed back the chair and got up from the table.

Anabelle hit two buttons: one turned off the screens and the other one started raising the shades. Bright sunlight streamed into the room, the contrast of its airiness felt foreign against the weight of the conversation that had taken place.

Kaelan followed, and the two of them walked back to the living room.

"Immy, prepare a room. Sam and Kaelan have agreed to stay for at least a couple days."

Imogen got up and disappeared down the hallway that led to the room where Sam and Sawyer had initially awoken.

"I'll go check out of our hotel and get our things. Are you good to stay without me?"

"I'm great," Sam answered sarcastically, but smiled at Kaelan anyway. "Be safe. See you when you get back. I'll deal with my sister."

Kaelan nodded to the women in the room, kissed her softly on the forehead, and left to complete his task.

Sam turned around to face Amira and Iyana. She took a deep breath.

"Alright, where did she go?"

The two women pointed towards the front door.

She stepped into the cool evening air and spotted Sawyer sitting on a bench off to the side of the main driveway.

"Plan on running away?" she called ahead so she could get Sawyer's attention.

"You could put it that way, my car will be here soon." Sawyer didn't look at her when she answered.

"So, that's it? Fuck the whole world, huh?" Sam gazed out at the view that Sawyer pretended to be fixated on.

Sawyer fidgeted with her fingers, holding them in her lap. "You could put it that way," she repeated monotonously.

"Interesting—"

"What is?" Sawyer snapped before Sam could finish.

"I don't know you, but I didn't imagine that my twin sister would be so selfish."

The words stung. She glared at Sam, who was no longer looking at her.

"Selfish? You think I'm selfish? I didn't *ask* for this!"

Sawyer stood up suddenly, drawing Sam's attention back to her — the two of them, face to face.

"I didn't ask to have magic. I don't want the responsibility of protecting humanity from demons. DEMONS! This doesn't even sound real." Sawyer was panting and screaming. The wind had picked up, carrying her voice across the open space.

"And once the veil comes down? Did the rest of humanity *ask* for it? Your friends? Your family? The little children who are off somewhere right now getting ice cream? Me — your *sister*?"

Sam's voice had stayed low and even-keeled; a stark comparison against the blustery wind and her sister's screaming. And Sawyer felt ashamed as she stood in tears while her sister stared at her with an unreadable expression. She wanted Sam as her sister, as much as she wanted nothing to do with these women or their magic and their cause.

"Sawyer, no one's keeping you hostage, and no one can make you stay if you don't want to," Sam ran her hand through her curly hair. "But I thought we were facing whatever came together."

"*You said that, not me.*"

The sound of wheels up the driveway stopped their strained conversation.

"I got to go; my car is here." Sawyer turned away from her sister and started to walk away.

"If you think you can go back to living life like a normal little girl while the world is ending around you, you're more deluded than I thought." The words echoed through her mind as she climbed into the car and drove away.

"I'll change your mind, sister," Samantha whispered to herself as she watched the red lights of the car disappear down the driveway. "Just wait and see."

Sam walked back into the house alone. Imogen, Iyana, Anabelle and Amira were sitting together in the living room.

"We only need one of them and I already like she sister more," Iyana continued as she walked in.

"We don't know that for sure though. What if, because they're twins, we need both?" Imogen was sitting with her legs over the side of the chair, swinging them as she waited for an answer.

"That's why we need to convince her to accept this, and quick." Sam flopped down in a seat. "She's gone, by the way. Called a car and just fucked off." She flung her arms exasperatedly into the air.

Iyana was failing to suppress a laugh.

"So, what do we do?" Sam looked at the group.

"Well, she's your sister," Amira offered.

"Who I met yesterday. Nope, actually, that was today. Who I met *today*. She's as much of a stranger to me as the rest of you are."

"Point made." Anabelle rubbed her temples in frustration. "Do we know how we could get her back? What happened when you were in the blue orb. Anything we could use from there?"

There was nothing in the visions that would help with bringing Sawyer back, but Sam recapped the experience for the rest of them anyway.

"I can try to talk to her again — go after her and see if distance from all of you will help."

Everyone nodded in agreement. Iyana got up and left the room, and when she came back, she dropped a set of keys into Sam's lap.

"You can take my car, but don' scratch my child." She winked and reclaimed her seat.

"Go to your sister. See if you can convince her. We'll work on getting the joining ceremony prepared, we'll do it even if it's just for you, but hopefully it's for both."

Imogen led her to the garage and Sam pressed the key in her hands, listening for the signature "beep beep" sound of the car identifying itself. Sam walked up to the midnight blue Mercedes-Benz and ran her hand over the side of the hood before getting into the car. She started the car and wiggled her shoulders with excitement at the purr of the engine.

"This is a *nice* car." She smiled at Imogen. "Wish me luck!"

"Good luck. You're gonna need it." Sam laughed and pulled out of the garage so she could go talk some sense into her sister.

The pitter-patter of raindrops brought Sawyer a modicum of tranquility, and before she knew it, she was sitting on the windowsill, pushing it open so she could smell the rain as it hit the grass and barely cooled cement.

Deep breath. One, two, three, four.
Hold. One, two, three, four.
Exhale. One, two, three, four.
Again.

She relaxed against the wall and curled her knees up to her chest. The rain was picking up pace, creating a misty spray that made its way onto her face. Sawyer closed her eyes and smiled her first real smile in days. She could hear people running in from outside, some laughing, others swearing. Car doors were being slammed shut, and the click-clack of heels on wet steps permeated the air. Most people were used to light rainfall, but with every passing minute, the showers intensified until it was a flat-out downpour. The harder it came down, the more people sought refuge indoors, and the more laughing and screaming echoed through the streets below her, until eventually the sound of the downpour drowned everything else out.

She absentmindedly checked her phone. She wanted to message her mother, to send her a paragraph-length plea for help, but the sight of the "compose message" screen was enough of a deterrent. There was no way she could explain what was happening. She didn't even understand it herself. So, Sawyer turned the phone face down and continued sitting in silence.

By the time the rain was over, her tank top was soaked all the way through. She removed the wet shirt, using it to semi-dry her face, which didn't work that well, before she dropped it in a ball on the floor and grabbed a sweatshirt. She picked up her phone again — missed calls and texts from Imogen, but nothing from Sam. *She doesn't have my number.* And she hadn't asked for Samantha's either. *But she would have gotten it from someone, if she had wanted to.*

Her thoughts drifted to her identical twin sister, and then ruminated on the fact that Sam knew about her magic and could even use it. She wasn't surprised, or even a little freaked out, when the others had tried to recruit her. She'd smiled and produced a snowstorm from her palm instead of running away.

Sawyer wasn't used to comparing herself so closely to anyone else, but how could she not. They looked the same, sounded the same, and in a lot of ways, even moved the same. But Sam was intriguing and brave— when Anabelle had told them about the demons, Samantha didn't look phased at all. Even in their vision, she'd run into possible danger with nothing on her mind but collecting information to figure out their situation in hopes of getting them home.

Sawyer was used to being uniquely her own — there was no one else like her in the world. But now she had a twin, which made her one of two. She shook her head in an attempt to dislodge her thoughts. If *she* couldn't help but compare herself to Sam, other people would too.

She imagined how the others had, in all likelihood, talked about how she had a meltdown while Samantha remained stoic through it all. Samantha had complete control over her own magic, while Sawyer had no idea what she was doing. She wondered if they'd decided she wasn't worth the effort because they already liked her sister better.

They probably don't need me anymore anyway.

She thought back to Sam's little demonstration, jealousy making her body tingle.

New determination nestled its way into her, replacing her negative thoughts. Alert, she sat up in bed and rolled her shoulders back. Even if it was just this one time, she needed to try.

The movies always tell you to clear your mind, right? Focus. Okay, deep breath. Focus.

Nothing.

Of course, nothing happened. I need to figure out what I'm trying to do.

Sawyer took another deep breath, imagining a small flame floating in the middle of her palm, but nothing appeared. She adjusted her position, crossing her legs and rolled her shoulders back for a second time.

Lengthen your spine and concentrate. Relax.

Still nothing.

She tried for another half an hour, focusing intensely on producing *anything*, even the tiniest flicker of a flame. Eventually, she became too frustrated and exhausted by her failure. Defeated, she slipped on a pair of sneakers and headed out into the rain-chilled night.

12

A Lifetime Gig

SAWYER

The campus was relatively empty due to the rain. It was also extremely late, and a weeknight during finals week, so it wasn't uncommon for it to be so deserted. Sawyer walked until she found a bench, dried off the seat with a paper towel she'd rammed into a pocket, and sat down. Her phone was back in her room since she didn't want the distraction of checking to see if her sister had reached out. All she wanted to do was sit in the silence of the night.

The lilac, vanilla breeze from the blossoming cherry trees wrapped itself around her and Sawyer started to cry. Silent streams of salty tears ran down her face, and after a while, she didn't even bother wiping them away.

The crying lasted for ten minutes, and afterwards, Sawyer uncurled her legs to stretch, having pulled her feet up onto the bench when she'd initially sat down. She pulled the hood of the sweatshirt off, letting the wind toss her hair around. She was ready to go back to her room when she heard soft whimpering coming from directly ahead. There was something small standing in the shadows cast by the streetlight.

Sawyer got up from the bench and stepped a little closer to get a better look. A few seconds later, a skittish looking puppy hobbled forward. There was still a large gap between the two, and Sawyer was thankful because she didn't want to startle the injured pup.

"What's the matter, girl? Where's your owner?" Sawyer glanced around anxiously, realizing, for the first time, that this situation wasn't the safest one to be in. She hadn't told anyone where she was going and while this could just be a hurt animal, it could also be a ploy to get her back, or someone trying to attack her. She pulled her hands around herself and took a step in the direction of her house. The puppy whimpered again and hobbled a step closer to Sawyer.

"Are you lost?"

The dog tilted its head to the side and stared at her. She stared back for a moment, contemplating whether it was risky to trust that the puppy was alone. Sawyer stepped forward once more, deciding that anyone using an injured animal as a ruse would have already stepped out and ambushed her if that was the plan.

She was six feet apart from the puppy when the air around them became muggy and stifling, making it hard for her to breathe. The scent of the cherry blossoms morphed into a putrid odor of decay and sulfur.

For a split second, she was sure she saw the puppy smile, before its head snapped sharply to the other side and the exposed side of its neck opened up to reveal a blue, thick, serpentine tongue. It shifted its paws on the ground, kneading the un-moving cement underneath, as long, black, talons emerged from the tips. The puppy's fur was gone — it laid in piles around its body, and where it had previously clung to the dog, was now just blistered skin. The only thing that remained the same was the size and relative shape.

Sawyer stood motionless, watching the entire transformation. She didn't think she could move even if she wanted to — the feeling of dread had magnetized her feet to the ground. But when the monster's pupils flickered to glowing yellow, she took a step back.

The creature hissed, uncurling its tongue, and shot it across the dark with an unnatural speed, encircling Sawyer's ankle. She screamed as acid quickly burned its way through her pants, reaching her skin; her sister's warning kept replaying in her head.

Sam parked the car and got out, making her way towards Sawyer's sorority house when a piercing scream stopped her cold in her tracks. She couldn't figure out where it was coming from, so she cocked her head and listened carefully. Then spun around and took off towards it, realizing the sound was coming from behind her. Sawyer would have to wait.

She ran as quickly as her feet would take her, unsure of where she was going; she followed the screams using instinct. Sam rounded a corner and dashed up a small ramp. The scene she came upon flooded her with absolute horror.

Her sister came into view first, and in no time at all, Sam registered that the blood-curdling screams were coming from Sawyer, who was sprawled across the pavement. She was a few feet away from a creature that had its tongue latched around her ankle. Sam quickened her pace and called out for her.

As she twisted her head towards the sound of her name, another scream ripped out of Sawyer's throat. Her vision was starting to blur from the pain of the demon dog's tongue — the burning was unbearable, and struggling to free herself only seemed to make it worse. At the sound of Sam's approaching footfall, the creature started to retreat, dragging Sawyer with it.

When Sam was close enough to Sawyer, she materialized thin ice daggers and flung them towards the pair. The daggers got to Sawyer and the dog, a moment before Sam grabbed her arm — one of them hit the creature on its nasty, blue tongue causing it to recoil. It bellowed in pain before turning to Sam.

"What the fuck?" Sam was hoisting Sawyer off the ground, using her body to support her sister's weight.

She kept her eyes on the thing looking back at her while she dragged Sawyer to a large boulder near the top of the ramp. Setting her down, she turned back to the creature, now standing in the shadows.

"We need to get out of here." Sawyer's voice was raw from screaming. She sounded nothing like the woman she'd met earlier that day.

"I can't just leave it here, what if it attacks someone else?"

"Do you know how to kill a demon?!"

"No!"

Sawyer was still looking at the monster. "Then we need to go!" Her terror was at an all-time high, it was coming off her in waves.

"Wait, how do you know it's a de—" A fiendish laugh halted their conversation. The thing started running towards them when it crashed into an invisible shield that pulsed lavender on impact.

"The veil," Sam whispered, taking a few steps towards where the demon had stopped. "It has to be."

"And we have to leave! It can't pass through, let's go!" Sawyer begged. She was trying to get herself off the rock so she could drag herself and Sam to safety.

"But what if someone walks around the corner and it grabs them?" Sam started moving towards the demon who had started to salivate, tiny drops of its acidic drool searing the pavement.

Sam wrapped her fingers around a newly formed dagger as she advanced— if she couldn't kill it, maybe she could send it back to where it came from. She reached the veil, and threw her dagger directly at the demon dog when something yanked it out of the way.

The demon regained its footing and looked back into the shadows beyond the lamp post.

"Did you get it?" Sawyer asked from her distant position on the rock.

"No, something jerked it out of the way." Sam was leaning closer to the veil, squinting through the darkness as she tried to find whatever had saved the creature which was hissing at her again.

She shifted her attention from the shadows to the demon, determined to try again. She was so focused on finding out what was behind the trees, Sam didn't hear the sound of the Shuriken hurtling towards her until it was too late. It was made of shadows and pierced the veil, marring the unblemished skin of her face with a massive gash.

Sam screamed and dropped the dagger, her hand reflexively flying up to cradle her face. Blood was dripping through her fingers and down her elbow, a small pool starting to form below her.

"Sam!" Sawyer was calling for her, still unable to move from the boulder she was on.

The pain from the laceration made her woozy, but she steadied herself and peered into the darkness again.

A child emerged from the darkness and lingered at the end of the shadow. His orange eyes glowed like the demon dog's. He pulled on an invisible chain, and the dog obediently rushed back to him. His eyes never left Sam.

"It's not time yet." His voice was layered, like multiple people were speaking through him. The distorted sound of it repulsed Sam — she could feel it slithering over her skin.

She quickly materialized some spikes of ice and threw them through the veil, aiming at him. But he was faster than the dog and leaned to the left to avoid them, looking behind him as they sailed into the shadows.

"It's not time," he paused and stepped forward until the overhead streetlight illuminated the pointed edges of the teeth that made up his sinister grin. "Yet."

His orange eyes danced at the declaration. He stepped back into the shadow and disappeared, taking the demon dog with him.

Sam ran back to Sawyer, blood still flowing from her face. She pulled off her shirt and pressed it up against the bleeding wound.

"What the fuck was that?" Sawyer's voice trembled as she peered back at the empty shadows.

Sam shook her head. "Let's just, get out of here."

They didn't bother to go to Sawyer's room for her phone or belongings. Sam and Sawyer rushed to the car and started making their way back. They needed to warn the others that they had no idea what was coming for them all. And they needed to get the veil back up as soon as possible.

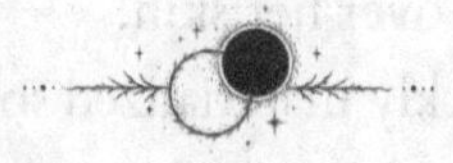

"We should stop at—" Sawyer paused.

"We should stop where?"

"*I was going to say at a hospital,* but *what the fuck would we even say?*"

Sam laughed, then winced at the pain. "Yeah, it probably makes more sense to just get back to the others anyway."

"Maybe they will have something to help." Sawyer had pulled her injured ankle into her lap and was trying to differentiate the burnt material of her pants from her skin so she could separate them.

They drove in heavy silence for a while.

"*How are you going to ask for their help when you ran away again?*" Sam asked, grateful for their ability to communicate telepathically so she could avoid adding to the already unbearable pain of her face.

"I have no fucking idea," Sawyer responded, causing Sam to chuckle mentally.

"*Turned into a real cuss pot over there, huh?*" Sam sent the tiniest smile her way.

"Sorry, I swear a lot when I'm overwhelmed." Sawyer looked out the window before she started talking again and Sam chuckled.

"Even if they don't help me, I'm in." She turned back to Sam, who kept her gaze on the street as she drove, her hand pressing the blood-soaked shirt to her face. "I can't be the reason things like that are able to come into our world. I don't even know what I would have done if you didn't show up when you did. And I'm betting whatever yanked it back wasn't as little as its pet. If we can't stop a puppy-sized demon, *how the fuck* are we going to stop anything else?"

Sam listened, not sure if she should tell Sawyer about the demon child who'd stood on the other end of the creature's invisible chain. She knew she had to tell her, but it might be better to wait until they were all back together before revealing the exact specifics of the fucked-up situation they were in.

"*Just make sure you're in for real this time. Something tells me that once we agree, it's a lifetime gig.*"

Sawyer didn't answer immediately. She took a deep breath and looked at her sister, steeling her resolve.

"If you're in, I'm in."

"Then we're in. And let's hope, for everyone's sake, that by the time we're prepared, we aren't too late."

Epilogue

She began stirring awake when she sensed the initial weakening of the veil. Her eyes shooting open the exact moment the Ethereal's blood hit the earth's surface. She blinked, her vision quickly adjusting, as she scanned the darkness, looking for him.

An eerie smile formed on her lips as she pushed open the door, inhaling the cool air and reveling in its moldy odor. She cracked her neck and rolled her shoulders backwards before stepping out.

Keres descended the staircase that opened up from the glass chamber where she had been sleeping. She enjoyed the feeling of the damp earth beneath her bare feet as she strode off the stairs onto the floor of the expansive cave. Gazing around, she examined the place where she'd spent this time waiting with her brother.

"Time to wake up, there's a lot that needs to be done and not enough time to do it."

Keberos heard her tiny voice echo through his head. He pushed open the glass door of his chamber, sauntering down the limestone staircase and across the cave so he could peer into the pair of irises that were the mirror image to his own.

When he came into view, she smiled diabolically. He smiled back at the maleficent twinkle in her eyes.

She was excited, and that excitement was steeped in destruction — it encouraged a sinister chuckle from Keberos that echoed through the cave.

"I'm awake, little sister. And I'm ready."

Acknowledgements

I have no idea where to begin! I started Primordial years ago and I've been working on it and avoiding it constantly, on and off since then. It's the first big piece of work I showed to my husband and it went from being a series, to a standalone, then back to a series again. Now here it is! Book one is finally complete.

As usual I want to thank my husband because without his encouragement, you wouldn't be reading anything from me at all. Then I have to shout out my parents and friends! To every single one of you who continues to show up to support me, you have no idea how impactful it is. Thank you so much.

To my beta readers Jessica, Jabari and Mrs. Dani D! You all helped me with this story so much and I appreciate your immeasurable feedback.

To my ARC readers, thank you for your ratings and reviews! And to my street team, you all are rockstars! I appreciate the support and help so much.

This story wouldn't be what it is without my amazing editor. Eisha, your work on this story was every thing I didn't know it needed. You definitely hurt my feelings a little in the beginning but you made the story better in the end! I can't wait to work with you on something new.

If you were wondering who does all the art. You have Zoe and Jazmin to thank for the beautiful cover, headers and scene breaks because I cannot draw to save my life. Zoe, thank you so much for bringing my project and every project so far, to life. I literally do not know how I would do this without you and I appreciate that you let me stress you out. Jazmin, I appreciate you letting me rope you into a last minute project especially with all my indecisiveness.

And lastly, I want to thank you – the reader. If you're here that means you've finished book one and I hope you liked it. You can hate it too, that's okay. Thank you anyway. Especially if you share it with someone or leave me a review. If you enjoyed the story, I hope you fell in love with the characters as much as I love writing them and I hope you come back to see what happens next.

The good news? I'm already working on book two.

About the author

Chia lives almost exclusively among star-flecked skies and dragon-guarded realms, where gravity is optional and impossibilities are simply plot twists waiting to happen. A longtime word-smith with a razor-sharp wit, she's happiest when inventing new worlds, and steadfastly ignoring the mundane one we all share.

 Off the page, Chia is as genuine as they come—quick to share a laugh, even quicker to share a cocktail, and always ready to champion another creative in the pursuit of their dreams.

Chia's writing is a nod to her roots, where characters come to life and imaginative, unpredictable stories unfold. Her books combine the thrilling awe of classic sci-fi with the magic and wonder of fantasy, leaving readers convinced that reality is, quite frankly, overrated.

Need a portal out of the ordinary? Chia's got you covered!

Also by

The Day the World walked into The Sea
Bougainvillea Isle

www.ingramcontent.com/pod-product-compliance
Lightning Source LLC
Chambersburg PA
CBHW010728310726
48971CB00009B/2773